SEASTRUCK

AND OTHER FANTASIES

SEASTRUCK
AND OTHER FANTASIES

MARILYN "MATTIE" BRAHEN

WILDSIDE PRESS

Dedicated to the spirit of the man who told me to keep writing, my mentor Ray Bradbury, and to my husband Darrell Schweitzer, who always "had my back," and still does.

CONTENTS

ALL IN THE GOLDEN AFTERNOON

He had only fallen asleep in the warm sun at the Oxford railroad station for a scant few minutes, but in that time, the manuscript, carefully packaged in brown paper and tightly bound with good string, had been stolen, along with a small brown hamper containing his lunch.

The food and wine were small loss compared to his printer's copy of *Alice's Adventures Under Ground.* He had labored on the book for over a year, since he originally recited it as a series of sketches to the Liddell children as he rowed them along the Thames on an expedition upriver. He had promised Alice, ten years old and dear to his heart, that he would write the tales of the fictional Alice and, now having completed that promise, he was traveling to arrange its publication.

But the manuscript was gone, and he felt a frantic sinking in his heart and took several long breaths, trying to calm himself. *Go about this logically,* he told himself. *You are, after all, a lecturer in mathematics.* The bench he had earlier seated himself on, before nodding off, was partially secluded by a tree and some bushes, a short distance from the station house. He studied the platform. The same two young ladies and their parents still milled about, keeping a close watch on their ample luggage and on a boy around Alice's age, who alternately stared at them sulkily or peered impatiently up the railroad tracks, trying to spot the train. It obliged him, appearing in the distance.

Beyond the waiting family, Charles noticed two new gentlemen, who hadn't been there prior to his own arrival. One carried a large portmanteau, which seemed filled to its seams with whatever it held. Still, Charles had no cause to confront them. He wondered what purpose he had now to even board the coming train without the manuscript and watched despondently as it pulled into the station.

A porter emerged first, then the carriage guard collecting the passengers' tickets. He escorted the family of five into the first carriage, nearly filling it, then waived the two strange gentlemen over to the second. The porter began loading the family's luggage into the baggage compartment.

Charles approached the station master, struggling to help the porter lift an oversized trunk. "Excuse me, gentlemen." They looked up, poised to hoist the obviously heavy piece. "I seem to have misplaced a brown-paper parcel and a lunch hamper while dozing. The parcel is extremely important." He hesitated. How could he accuse the late-arriving gentlemen of theft? Asking to search their belongings would be tantamount to that, wouldn't it? It was quite possible that someone else, unnoticed by the others, had come to the platform, taken his parcel and hamper, then left.

Yet he had to recover the manuscript or hope, at least, that the thief considered it worthless and discarded it. It might be found by someone kind enough to return it, Charles's name and address clearly printed on the wrapper, in case of such loss.

The station master answered him reluctantly. "Did you search thoroughly for them, sir?" The porter ignored him, saying *"Now!"* Both men heaved upward, swinging the trunk into the baggage area. The porter jumped up, pushed it further in, jumped down, pulled the sliding door closed and secured it.

"They were on the bench right beside me. The parcel contains a manuscript I've written. I was carrying it to my publisher, Macmillan, in London."

"Well, I don't like to say it, sir," the station master began, only to be interrupted by a loud feminine scream, followed a high-pitched stream of hysterical complaints. "What now?" He rose stiffly.

One of the gentlemen emerged from the train, opening the compartment door and calling to the guard. "There's an animal running loose in our carriage, sir. A large striped tomcat, from the looks of it."

"Now, what the devil..." the train man groused, and boarded the carriage. A commotion sounded within, and the cat, orange with large black stripes, bounded from it and onto the platform, its teeth firmly clamped on the string of a wrapped parcel. It dragged it along as it skittered away toward the bench, tree and bushes and disappeared beneath the shrubbery.

"My manuscript!" Charles raced after it, parting the leafy branches to forage in the undergrowth and triumphantly reclaim *Alice's Adventures Under Ground.*

The station master caught up with him, winded with exertion. "Would that be the missing parcel, sir?"

"It is, and I'm delighted to have it back!"

"Can't say I understand how it got aboard the train, much less the cat."

"The important thing is that it's been returned."

"Do you think the cat dragged it off the bench, sir, and then snuck on board with it?"

"I...I couldn't really say, now could I? But if you find a small brown hamper under some foliage," (he drew apart more shrubbery, which revealed only leaves and dirt), "it might support that theory. I doubt that the cat could have dragged *both* the parcel and hamper onto the train without being seen."

"Unlikely," the station master agreed. "In that case, sir, do you think a thief has boarded at my station?"

Charles hesitated. "I couldn't say that either, sir. I slept through the theft and can't vouch for whether teeth, claws or fingers were employed."

"Then you don't want an investigation?"

He shook his head. "I'd rather not. The hamper wasn't valuable. This was." He held up the manuscript.

"Charles Lutwidge Dodgson, Christ Church?" the station master read. "Well, sir, we'll return the hamper to you, if it's found. In the meanwhile, I'll warn the carriage guard to keep an eye out for persons with a pilfering nature on the train. Will you be boarding, sir?"

"Yes, now that my reason for traveling has been restored."

He handed the guard his ticket and took the remaining seat in the first carriage, introducing himself to the family sharing the compartment. As the train finally pulled out, Charles relaxed by the window, holding the parcel alertly and protectively against himself, and entertaining the young boy and his sisters with a story or two, while their parents listened, amused.

At the next station, the two men he had seen on the platform at Oxford disembarked. Shortly afterwards, in the compartment they had vacated, new passengers found an empty lunch hamper. They gave it to the carriage guard at the following station stop; he returned it to its rightful owner.

Charles, both manuscript and hamper in hand, dashed madly to the station eatery to purchase some refreshments and quickly back to reboard the train before it started up again. On the platform, the station master of that stop, an elderly man with immense white whiskers and a curious habit of wrinkling his nose, held a large, opened pocket watch in his hand, haranguing the carriage guard: "You're four minutes late, sir! Whatever delayed you?"

Charles reentered his compartment swiftly and took his seat, gazing quietly out the window. It was then that he noticed another enormous orange and black-striped tomcat, sitting on that platform and preening itself. He pointed it out to the boy beside him. "There was another striped puss, nearly identical to this one, at the Oxford Station."

"Was there? I hadn't seen it, sir."

The tom looked up, turned its head, and stared back at the mystified author.

The train wheels began to creak, and the cat continued to gaze at him, turning its head the other way as Charles, at the window, passed by it.

In the few seconds before the cat disappeared from Charles's view, it grinned at him.

After a moment of surprise, Charles grinned back.

"No matter," he told the boy. "Cats like that have a tendency to appear unexpectedly. You might very well see it again someday soon."

The train headed toward its final destination as the sun began setting, streaking colors across the sky.

AFERTERE'S EYES

Carina lay beneath him, the most beautiful woman in the land, Alowyn thought…even outshining the fine rich ladies he had once glimpsed at the royal courts of Drissandere. Her long ebony hair swelled out against the crushed meadow grass as they grappled in the humid summer night, all hands, legs and lips, swaying and squirming, hidden by the tall untouched grass surrounding them.

Carina's black eyes flashed, passionate emotion building in them. She caught a swath of Alowyn's pale blonde hair in her hand, pulling his face down, his ardent blue eyes level with her own. His full warm lips met hers. Arching suddenly, her slender body slowly relaxed under his as his strong hands clutched her shoulders. He shuddered, his slick skin merging with her own, his body heavy, sated, against her.

They rested, stroking each other, sharing an extra kiss or two in the afterglow until their strength returned, then Carina retrieved their clothing, flinging Alowyn his. She was dressed before him, and as he finished, pulling on his shirt, she drew the ring off her right forefinger and handed it to him.

He held it gingerly, examining it in the full moonlight. Its two emerald stones sparkled strangely. A golden glint, like a pupil, seemed to flame within each stone's center.

"Is it magical?"

"My great grandmother named it Afertere's Eyes. When it's passed on to someone you love, it grants each new owner an honorable wish."

"And when you received it? What did you wish?"

"I wished—" she started, her cheeks dimpling, "—for true love!" She laughed, pouncing on him, seeking his lips with boisterous determination.

He fended her off, holding the ring aloft. "Stop! You'll make me drop it!"

She sat up, smoothing her skirt around her raised knees. "You're always so serious. I would have found it, had you dropped it."

"Are your eyes that keen at night?" He reached for her and pulled her down to complete the kiss he had thwarted. They broke apart and sat up, Alowyn's arm around her.

Alowyn stared at the dark-haired girl he had deserted his own family for. He studied the ring.

"My betrothal gift to you," she said. "To you who left your home and kin to learn the music of the Wandering Folk and to become my husband."

"How does this magic work?"

Carina paused, quietly meeting his gaze. Tangles of damp hair fell heavily across her eye. "It must be worn before you can make your wish upon it. Worn on the right forefinger, which leads to the heart."

He smiled at her tutorial tone. "And if it doesn't fit that finger?"

"Then it isn't meant for you, and you have to give it back."

Alowyn slid the ring along his right forefinger. It passed the knuckle easily, fitting perfectly. Carina sighed her relief. "Now shut your eyes and make your wish, asking that Afertere grant it."

"Out loud?"

"It doesn't matter…but I would like to hear it."

Alowyn closed his eyes, concentrating, pale brows furrowing. "I wish to become the greatest musician, so great, the gods themselves will covet my music. May Afertere grant my wish." He lifted his eyelids, and laughed, delighted with her gift. "Have I asked for too much?"

Carina stared back, shivering in the cooling night air. "I don't know. We'll have to wait and see. No one has ever wished for such a thing before."

* * * *

The Chieftain of the Wandering Folk tied thongs of leather about their wrists, declared them mated, and welcomed Alowyn into the tribe through marriage.

Wine flowed lavishly as the Folk toasted the new bride and groom, then laughing banter and fine belches filled the early evening as they gathered round tables laid out with the wedding feast of cheese, bread loaves, slabs of roasted meat, and fruit. Night came on. They lit torches and lanterns, and passed around tankards of warm ale to the adults, and cups of sweet cider to the youngsters.

Alowyn took his flute and drew it to his lips. A piping melody emerged, as sweet as birds' song in the dawn. The Wandering Folk joined in. Soon the sounds of guitar and fiddle, tambourine and drum swelled into the night air. What began as a light refrain grew rapidly into a quick tempo jig. Dancers filled the meadow clearing where the Folk had camped and now celebrated. Their feet stepped in lightning rhythm. Their faces flushed with sweat and delight. Swirling and twirling fetchingly was Carina. The skirt of her silken green wedding dress danced upon the air around her legs, showing off the shapely, sturdy contours beneath the fabric.

The spirited music faded to an end, and tapping, kicking, leaping feet ebbed to stillness as exhausted dancers sat or sprawled on the damp grass. As Alowyn tuned his mandolin, a hush fell over the camp, and he began to sing a haunting madrigal of love gone awry.

Carina tucked her legs beneath her skirt, leaning on one hand on the grass, listening. Alowyn bent over his mandolin, a waterfall of sparkling notes cascading from its strings, his voice more resonant and richly controlled than it had ever been before.

The last verse Alowyn sang drifted off into the night wind, poignant and sad, and his fingers plucked an exquisite finale from the mandolin. The momentary quiet was quickly replaced by fervent prolonged applause. High praise from the Wandering Folk, famous across the entire continent for their own music and dancing.

The deep baritone of Sofar, Carina's father, interrupted the enthusiastic clapping and noisy hooting approval. "Your performance skill seems to have increased at least threefold." He sat near the central fire pit, his tapestried robe, threaded with gold and silver, glimmering in its light.

His eyes spied the gleam of the emerald ring on Alowyn's right forefinger, but he said nothing further, simply glancing at his daughter with raised brows.

"Only enhanced by thoughts of love and other skills," Alowyn answered with a sly wink. A gale of ribald laughter erupted among the Folk. Sofar smiled, but didn't join in.

* * * *

Within one year, Alowyn's extraordinary performances, sought by the richest nobles, brought him widespread acclaim. Gold and favors were liberally bestowed upon him. Gold filled the pockets and purses of the Wandering Folk as well, as they accompanied him both in travels and instrumentally, from castle to castle, from stronghold to stronghold. Carina often danced to the beautiful music Alowyn coaxed from a variety of instruments, his abilities increasing with each cycle of the moon. He need only be shown an instrument and, given an hour, played it fluently. His expertise now extended beyond flute and mandolin, to harp, guitar, fiddle, and harmonium.

But if Carina's fine looks and captivating fluid dancing were the wick to Alowyn's flame, she went unnoticed in the comparison. The High King Yuoric soon ordered Alowyn to journey to Drissandere, to reside at court, and to study and perform with the royal musicians.

Privately, the message-bearer confided to Alowyn that only Carina could accompany him to the High Court. The Wandering Folk took the news with snide humor. They, too, had an aversion to the simpering manners of royalty. Good-naturedly, they helped Carina and Alowyn prepare supplies for their five-day journey, and the Chieftain himself gifted them with two strong mares to carry them to Drissandere.

Once at court, Carina found herself surrounded by finely-dressed ladies who advised her insistently on style and etiquette. She soon resembled them in dress and manner, fitting in outwardly. But in her heart, she missed the wide spaces, the travels, and the unencumbered freedom of the Wandering Folk.

Alowyn, fawned and fussed over, settled in eagerly, spending many hours with the court musicians, discussing theory, learning from them, and performing with them.

But whatever he was taught, he soon exceeded those who taught him. Gossip flitted around Drissandere: Alowyn was either genius or bewitched, perhaps both. Such talk broadened his mystique and popularity, fueling his creative ego. He began to compose original music, works borne of fiery visions that assaulted his brain and left him no peace until they were written down in musical script, a skill King Yuoric's court composer had instructed him in.

A date and time were set for him to perform his brilliant work before the court. In the throne room, they erected a second dais to accommodate Alowyn and a small quintet of accompanying musicians.

Finely-attired lords and ladies took their seats expectantly, and Alowyn, seated beside a golden harp, motioned the other musicians to begin.

His fingers plied the harp strings, and an achingly exquisite melody arose. Behind him, flute and harmonium lent subtle accents to his sure handiwork. The audience sighed as the music caressed their ears and souls, and Carina sat in the front row, tears flowing from her eyes.

Then chaos erupted. Five men and four women fell heavily from their chairs in the audience, fainting. Servants carried them away. A muted buzz of consternation filled the throne room, quieting as the program resumed, undisturbed to the final note played.

It was later discovered that all nine fainters suffered from long-standing physical malaises, and that all nine were healed completely by week's end. Alowyn's music, the court whispered, was the cure.

The High King Yuoric brought Alowyn before him. "The nobles are arguing whether your music stems from divine or demonic influences," Yuoric, with a gleam in his royal eyes, confided. "I do not care myself, as long as the effect it has is for the good!"

Alowyn replied with quiet earnestness, "It is the gods' influence, my liege."

Yuoric smiled. "Perhaps. I like a good tonic as well as the next man. You might, however, in your future compositions, create music a bit less stimulating?"

"As best I can, my liege," Alowyn promised.

But at his next performance, nearly half the audience fell down in religious ecstasies, calling out the names of gods, some even taking on the persona of a god or goddess, singing praise for Alowyn's music in unnatural voices before losing consciousness. Alowyn played on as if nothing untoward was happening, even when his accompanists set aside their instruments in confusion and terror.

Upon awakening, none of the afflicted remembered their words or movements while entranced. Nor did any healing or other beneficial effect follow their entrancement.

King Yuoric, unaffected by the music, called for his High Priest, Maelric.

Maelric touched Alowyn's chest and forehead simultaneously, chanting a long string of indecipherable words, and rocking back and forth with his eyes raised to the heavens. He slowly steadied himself, staring with both horror and adoration at Alowyn.

"He is beloved of the gods!" Maelric shouted, releasing Alowyn. "And most favored by Afertere, the goddess of music and dance, for through his music, he honors her."

Carina, standing nearby, stared down at the golden ring Alowyn wore, its twin emerald stones, and the strange golden mote within each.

Maelric took sudden notice of her. "It's said that the Wandering Folk are favored by the gods. While composer Alowyn is not of their blood, his lady is. Have you bewitched him, my lady? Perhaps called upon Afertere to bless him?"

"No…no!" Carina stammered.

"Then you must relinquish him," Maelric said in a tone that held no sympathy for her fears or the suffering she felt. "He no longer belongs to you. Afertere is the favorite of Nekeras, the father of the gods, who has decreed that any mortal she covets is beholden to her until released by death. Alowyn will be anointed and cared for by my priesthood, as one cherished by the gods. Afertere has claimed him."

"But he is my husband!"

"No longer," Maelric repeated. "Would you defy Afertere?"

Carina turned beseechingly to Alowyn. Her heart chilled, seeing what remained of him. His eyes gazed into her own without feeling, and then turned upward into their sockets, showing empty white. A frightening golden aura shone like dust motes around the edges of his open lids.

King Yuoric laid a gentle hand on her shoulder. "My heart goes out to you, my lady. You are most welcome to remain here at court, under my protection, if you wish. But neither you nor I can fight the will of the gods."

Carina gripped the unmoving Alowyn's right hand. "This is my betrothal ring to him," she explained. "I would have it back."

She tugged and pulled, but the ring would not slide free.

"It is not meant to be," Maelric told her.

"Perhaps it is meant to stay with him," Yuoric said soothingly, "that a part of you will stay with him as well."

"Alowyn!!" Carina cried out, as if her shriek could pierce the veil over his heart. But he neither heard nor responded, as Maelric grasped his arm and led him without resistance from the throne room.

* * * *

Carina refused Yuoric's offer. He provided funds and an escort and returned her to her people. Her solitary arrival went unquestioned, for the Wandering Folk have long ears and glib tongues. Over tankards of ale, Sofar had discussed Carina's transfer of Afertere's Eyes to Alowyn, had discussed his fears concerning Alowyn's wish upon it. As events now played themselves out, Sofar's fears proved well-founded.

Further word came that Maelric's priests had built a temple for Alowyn, where supplicants could hear his strange musical renderings and pray to Afertere, yet no man nor woman among the Wandering Folk ever advised Carina to abandon her loyalty to her lost husband. The way of the Folk was to mate for life.

In their travels, the Folk ofttimes passed near the Temple of Afertere where Alowyn resided, meeting with pilgrims coming and going from the shrine, seeking cures or craving the ecstasies Alowyn's performances often brought. Many reported that his music frightened them—discordant and powerful, seeming to split their very souls open and fill them with its sound. "It's meant for the gods' ears, I suppose," one pilgrim told them, "but no matter. When I woke from my daze, my leg no longer pained me and could bear my weight!"

When they passed closely enough, Carina traveled to the temple to visit Alowyn. Sometimes his gaze settled on her and he seemed to know her. Once, he smiled, then sighed. Several times, he wept. But then his music called. His eyes would cloud over; recognition fled like a small bird that would not be contained, even by a warm, imploring, outstretched hand. He would sit by the harp, or grasp the mandolin, or raise a flute to his lips, his sightless eyes upon the statues of Afertere and the other gods that stood within the temple, and he would play.

And so Carina would leave him, her heart still burdened, but glad to have seen him and shared what little communion they could.

Ten years passed. Her faithfulness both a blessing and a curse, she had aged, no longer strong, but her frailty held an aura of quiet patient beauty about it. A great weariness wore her down, and a desire to be with and commune with Alowyn, in whatever way she could, grew within her.

The Wandering Folk were traveling in the opposite direction, and so she saddled a horse one night and rode alone towards Drissandere.

She reached the Temple of Afertere as the sun rose, its rays bathing the marble-columned entrance. Carina stepped into the dark interior, empty save for a lone figure hunched over a harp, asleep against its frame.

She stared sorrowfully at the man, now aged and disheveled, whom she had never ceased to love. His hair, once blonde and shimmering in rich waves, was thin and white, matted and filthy upon his head, his clothes, soiled remnants of finery ill-cared for.

"Alowyn," she whispered.

He stirred, his head lifting. "Carina?"

He had spoken her name!

"Yes! It's me! Do you remember me, Alowyn?"

"Long ago, in a dream I had nearly forgotten."

"I have never abandoned the love I have for you," she said simply, glad again to share her heartmost feeling.

"I cannot remove the ring," he said dully, "nor the wish I made upon it."

"Then play for me. I cannot blame Afertere for loving you," she answered, glad for the shadows that hid her tears, "You are worthy of the love of a goddess. Play for me and let me pray to Afertere."

Even in the dusky chamber, she saw joy suffuse his face. With trembling hands, he grasped the harp. Music swelled from its strings. Major chords mixed with minor melodies. Rhythms switched—fast, moderate, slow as a dirge. Notes clashed, stood alone, and harmonized with other notes. Somehow, the seemingly incongruous composition melded together, built upon itself, and fit itself into place. From beginning to middle to end, it carried the thundering strength and the airy laughter of the gods conjoined.

Alowyn let his hands fall from the harp.

Carina, eyes still shut, still upon her knees, head bent in supplication, finished her prayer to Afertere. She lifted her head. "Your finest work," she said, through tears of amazement, for she had understood, and the work was beautiful.

"What did you pray for?" he asked.

"It doesn't matter. A prayer never granted."

He stepped slowly over to her and took her hand in his ringed right hand, bringing it to his lips and kissing it. "Forgive me," he said, and his arms went around her, drawing her close. "I have never forgotten. Deep within, you are remembered and cherished. But the visions of the gods come upon me and mask all memory. It is the price I pay for the wish."

Against his embrace, Carina felt sharp despair sting the final remnant of her hope. "Afertere," she called out, "why have you never heard my prayer? You are the patron goddess of dance and of music. Will you never end our pain? I shall never dance as wondrously as you, nor shall Alowyn sing or perform as wonderfully as you. But can you not restore us in some way that Alowyn and I might sing and dance together once more, and both of us pay tribute to you?!"

Silence and darkness.

She pulled away from Alowyn's arms. "I dare not return to you again," she said. "Each parting becomes more painful. Good-bye, my Alowyn. Remember me, as I shall you."

She walked woodenly towards the portico.

"Afertere!" Alowyn shrieked into the darkness. "I beseech you! Is there not a way in which we both may glorify you!?"

A light grew, warm and golden, casting shadows, filling the chamber with inhuman radiance. Carina turned back and stared at the stately female figure from which the radiance emanated. The goddess—for it could be no other—stood before the marble statue cast in her likeness, a cold and drab icon compared to her brilliance. The delicate drapery of her gown seemed spun from stars, her hair, the color of the sun at midday. And her eyes! Green as meadow grass with glimmers of molten gold at their core. Her lips were pale as she spoke, her voice held the timbre of a different world, a different time. "There is a way," Afertere said. "A way in which Alowyn can create a different eternal music, and you can dance an eternal dance. But you must sacrifice the forms in which you now clothe your souls." The goddess paused and regarded Carina knowingly, almost, it seemed for a second, wryly. "Will you accept both sacrifice and transformation?"

Carina knelt before Afertere, eyes shut, hands clasped forward. "I accept!"

She felt a hand, long, thin, and warm, upon her shoulder, and knew it was Alowyn's.

"Wait," he said, and to Afertere, "Is there no other way?"

The goddess turned to him. Her eyes seemed to soften with empathy. "How can there be? You have been touched by the gods; your wife has borne heroic suffering for the sake of the gods' will. Were I to restore you to your mortal lives, they would be tainted by the past and bitter, walking among mortals, outcast, neither belonging with them nor any more with the gods."

"Will we know one another, Carina and I?" Alowyn's hand clasped Carina's. A small tug, and she rose to her feet beside him.

"Yes," Afertere replied. "You shall know one another intimately."

"Then I accept also, and give you my trust and faith."

Alowyn drew Carina to him for one last mortal kiss. They drank hungrily of each other, their long-parched thirst finally sated.

As they embraced, their skin began to tingle, dissolving without pain. For both, their fleshy covering seemed replaced by something cool and soothing. But, for Alowyn, the coolness was fluid and in motion. For Carina, the coolness was light, nearly without substance, yet it, too, had direction and motion, as her essence danced within it.

* * * *

The lovers vanish from the story at the end. But those of us with sight and ears to sense hidden magic might chance upon the signs and recognize them.

Alowyn became a wide brook running through a forest that still shades the land where Drissandere once rose in all its finery. The brook still sings upon the stones and the water currents, and beasts and birds of the forest come and lend their music to its own.

Carina is the wind that still dances through the trees and stirs the leaves of that forest.

They are still there, and shall remain there, forever.

Yes, sit beside the brook within the forest that once bordered lost Drissandere. Listen. The branches of the trees along its bank may start to weave, their leaves swirling as the wind leaps and dances to the singing of the brook.

BABY MINE

I was told that Elsa was an Alaskan Husky pup when I adopted her in the late spring of 1998 from the Winnebago Indians at the Black River Trading Post roadside stand off the highway. I was driving from my job at the health spa that Friday to my apartment in Wittenberg, Wisconsin and had stopped there many a time before, as it's about halfway home and the gas and convenience mini-mart are across the side road. The stand has good vegetables and fruit for sale along with the Native American crafts for the tourists. But this time they had a sign that read, "Free Puppy— Needs Good Home."

I fell in love with Elsa the moment she stood up, frantically trying to get my attention, inside the cage Bart Haranga had housed her in. Bart, of the Potawatomi tribe of the Winnebagos, ran the stand. He came over to me and lifted the pup out. He said, "She likes you. Why don't you give her a home?"

"I don't know, Bart. I've never had a dog. Where did you get this puppy?"

He held the squirming pup firmly. "Foundling. Abandoned in the woods near the Black River Falls. I think someone's bitch had a small litter and they only kept one of the offspring. At any rate, this poor thing would have died if I hadn't rescued her. But I've got too many dogs as it is. Why don't you take her?"

He put her in my arms and darned if that little heartbreaker didn't calm right down, nuzzling my chest and neck and giving me that wide-eyed look. Temptation overcame my reluctance. I was divorced and had sold my house. I had no children and the apartment felt lonely. The pup's blue eyes penetrated straight to my heart, as if beseeching me to nurture her.

Bart stroked her soft white silver fur and said, "She needs love. She looks barely weaned. She'll make a good watchdog when she's grown, Carol."

I studied the puppy and then Bart. We were once almost lovers, after my divorce from Peter. Bart was attractive, 29 years old, never married. He was two years older than me, and we had met at a dance in Wittenberg, but I was too skittish about any relationship after Peter dumped me and moved to Florida, when I was 23. Three years of marriage down the drain. When Bart tried to court me little more than a year later, I just wasn't ready for another man that way.

But I did need to feel love, and the puppy nestling in my arms felt like love. "Umm, I don't even know how to train a dog, Bart."

"I'll come over after work and bring puppy chow and newspaper. I'll teach you. Look, she loves you."

The dog was licking my face, its little tongue raspy. "You're just looking for an excuse to get on my good side, Bart."

"Can't blame me for trying. Come on, Carol. I'll just help you get acclimated to the puppy. She just needs a mother right now. And a name." He looked at me with those dark, earth-brown eyes, his hair richly brown and just shy of long, his smile sincere, trustworthy. "I'll even pay for her food."

"Damn, Bart, I think I've fallen in love."

"With me or the pup?"

"With the puppy. Okay, I'll see you tonight. But give me some food for the dog to take back now, so I can feed her if you're late."

Bart put her back into the cage, took a few cans of wet dog food and hauled everything to my car, loading them in the back seat. Then he bagged the produce I'd selected, but refused to take any money. "So what are you going to name her?"

I gave him a cautious smile, still uncertain about taking the pup. "Well, I always wanted to name a daughter Elsa, but didn't have one. So I guess I'll call her Elsa."

"Nice name. Okay, I'll see you and Elsa tonight at 7:30 p.m., soon as I'm done here. Give her some milk if she won't eat the soft food. I'll stop and pick up some proper puppy chow."

* * * *

Elsa was easily trained. I walked her early in the morning and once at night and she never made a mess after the first week. She also loved the toys I bought her and sleeping on my bed at night, although she would paw me as if nursing and I worried that she'd been weaned too early. Bart came over once every weekend to check her progress and probably to check on his own with me. It became a routine, and his presence was becoming enjoyable. We'd watch movies or play cards and he'd act the perfect gentleman. When he left, he'd give me one gentle kiss and scratch Elsa's head.

But the third weekend held a surprise which neither of us expected. Elsa had been asleep on the rug while we watched TV. The sun had gone down, night came and I turned on the living room lights. Then Bart and I went into the kitchen to make some coffee. A minute later, we heard a baby crying, sounding close.

"What the heck?" Bart said.

"I don't know anyone in the building with a baby. Someone with one must be visiting." But the crying continued, and seemed to be coming from my living room. We started back there, steaming cups in hand, and put them on my coffee table. "Must be directly upstairs."

"Where's Elsa?"

I looked around. "She must have wandered off. She was just there, under the table."

The cry came again, and Bart got up to search for Elsa and froze by the side of the sofa, staring at the floor hidden behind its right arm. "Carol. Look!"

I did. A naked baby lay on the floor, its piercing blue eyes frightened and its silver white hair long and fine against the carpet as it wailed and shivered. A girl child, reaching out its small arms to me.

I reacted instinctively, picking her up. "Oh, God! Where did she come from?"

He stayed silent for a long minute, and then murmured, "I'll get a towel to wrap her in." He went into my bathroom, bringing back a fluffy towel to warm the baby in. But before he covered her completely, he examined her feet. Watching, I sucked in my breath: the baby's feet didn't have soft human skin. It had the pads of a canine.

"What is this?" I asked, "And where's Elsa?"

He hesitated before answering, looking at me directly, reluctant and worried. "This is Elsa, Carol. I've heard of these things, but never saw one before."

"How can this baby be Elsa?"

"Carol, listen to me. There are legends about this. And if I'm right, we have a hard task ahead of us."

I listened. It was hard believing what he said.

* * * *

Bart told me of a sort of reverse werewolf. Wolves are very much like humans: they love, they form family groups, they work together, and they are loyal to each other. They aren't blood-thirsty or violent by nature; they kill their prey for sustenance, never for sport. They respect it and keep its numbers thriving, so that the balance of nature is maintained. And as for their attitude towards mankind, they're both wary and curious about us, knowing us to be superior creatures and possibly more dangerous than any other animal. And so, most of the wolves avoid humans, a species they don't normally trust.

But according to the legends, some wolves became attracted to humanity, so much so, that they would steal among us and shed their wolf pelts and walk in the guise of humans, but only during a full moon when its light allowed that transformation. Then they would clothe themselves in our garments and appear to strangely question the men and women they met and sniff out our ways. Sometimes they became adept at passing as humans. People would make mention of a solitary woman who appeared now and then in town, wandering and mysterious, or a curious man who would nose into late night conversations. And sometimes there was talk of their quiet invitation to bed them and taste their pleasures. But in the morning, they vanished, although they might appear on another night in another month to the same lover, saying they had suddenly had to journey on unexpectedly, but now they had returned, promising to be as faithful as they could be. But they never stayed for more than a season; they knew they couldn't truly mate with us.

Bart called them by a Winnebago name I couldn't pronounce. "They are drawn to humans," he said, "but they know they are wolves, a cousin, but not a brother or sister, and that they cannot live among us as a human. And so their human lover one day wonders why he or she has been abandoned, but it wasn't because the wolf didn't care. The wolf did care, but it knew it must leave its lover for its lover's sake. And once they know this, they know they cannot shift again and must accept their wolf nature completely and leave humans be."

I asked, "What has this got to do with us and with Elsa?"

Bart sat with me on the sofa; I held the baby.

Bart nodded, as if agreeing with something he was thinking. "Carol, we have to find another wolf mother. Sometimes a she-wolf bears a child if she lies with a man. They say a human woman can also bear the child of a transformed male wolf. There are legends about that. But the child always dies and sometimes the mother, too." He shook his head. "Carol, I'm really sorry about this."

"So what do we do now?" I looked again at the baby's feet. "This is unbelievable."

"I know. We'll have to care for Elsa until I talk with the medicine man of my people. The legends say a transformed child-wolf can only be human during the full moon, and according to the lore she must go back to the wild or she'll die."

He took his cell phone from his pocket and dialed the medicine man. They talked for a while. He gave Bart the name and number of another tribal elder, and then Bart hung up. He told me that on the following weekend, when Elsa was once again a wolf—for wolf was what she was and not a dog—we would try to return her to her people.

* * * *

Bart drove us to a forested area farther north in Wisconsin. I held the wolf pup in my arms as we were met by an elderly female Winnebago tribeswoman who led us further into the woods, far away from any marked path. There she instructed me to put Elsa down before a huge tree and made me move away from her. Bart and I were told to stand at nearby trees, and the woman shook tobacco out of a large pouch into our hands. She then went over to Elsa and scattered the tobacco on the ground before the wolf pup.

I watched anxiously for Elsa to bolt, to run away or run to me, but she didn't. She sat down on the leaves and earth, as obedient as a trained dog, watching as the old woman began to sing in Winnebago. She also brought a rattle and moved it rhythmically to her singing, pointing it at Bart and me.

Bart instructed me, "Scatter the tobacco in your hands around the trees and call out to the spirits to have pity on Elsa. Tell the spirits that you are pleading for Elsa to be returned to her true family."

I stared at him.

"Do it, Carol." He pointed at the medicine woman. "She's 'calling down the thunder,' the power of the sky, the power of nature. Only that power can return Elsa to her true form permanently." Bart's eyes pleaded for my understanding. That there were realities beyond those we call normal, and only acceptance could make the magic work.

I flecked the tobacco around the tree we stood beside, and gazed at the pup who had stolen my heart. I had to give her up, caught in a mystery I barely believed in and yet had to believe in.

My mouth dry, I swallowed to moisten it, and I began: "I call down the thunder! Please protect my baby, whom You only let me love for the shortest time." My voice strengthened as a strange breeze seemed to swirl about me. "Please send her another mother to love her as I would have. Please do not leave her alone. Please bring her back to her wolf family!"

Bart scattered his own tobacco and let out a stream of musical words, his voice rising and falling, but I could not understand them, for they were in the Winnebago language.

And then something extraordinary occurred. Elsa began to whimper. I almost ran to her, but Bart quickly stopped me. From out of the woods, a full-grown wolf emerged, halted, and looked at the medicine woman and then at Bart and me. She slowly loped up to me in the forest clearing, leaned back on her hind legs, and then stood up again. She lifted her silver-furred head and bayed in a howl, its pitch unique, melodic. Somewhere in the distance, other wolves answered her. She gazed directly at me, her blue eyes penetrating.

The she-wolf—I knew the wolf was female—turned and trotted to Elsa. The pup greeted her eagerly, nuzzling against her underside seeking her nipples. The wolf licked Elsa tenderly and swiftly grasped her by the scruff of her neck, lifting her, claiming her as her own.

I wanted to run to the pup, to stroke her, a farewell, a goodbye. I involuntarily called her name. "Elsa."

The wolf-mother turned halfway, her eyes once more on my own, Elsa limply hanging by her scruff, acceptance in her posture, letting this new mother take her to their den. And then the wolf and Elsa disappeared through the thick woods.

The Winnebago medicine woman came over to Bart and me. "This is good," she said. "The child has returned to its true parent." She smiled sadly at me. "You are lonely. You need to have a true child of your own to love."

I nodded.

We walked silently along the forest path back to our cars and parted ways.

* * * *

Bart and I became closer after this. He finally won my love. We now have two sons and a daughter, our true children. Our daughter, of course, was named Elsa.

For years, I thought of the wolf puppy, and I became an advocate for the wolves. Last year, we took the children to a nature reserve where they could watch the wolves from a distance. And as we watched, one female with striking blue eyes and white silver fur came close to us and stood there. She gazed directly at me with open canine curiosity and then turned, moving off, not looking back.

CALL OF THE DRUM

Western Kenya, an autumn night in the last year of the seventeenth century.

The Lumbwa gathered in the clearing beyond the forest, forming a circle, the old women tending a row of fires within it. The full moon shone on the Kenyan grassland, adding its own clear light. The grain had been harvested, and now the Ngoma would be held. The dance held a special significance for Wamboi. She had become a woman, and now her eyes searched for Kitau.

She felt alluring in her oiled, embroidered, leather mantle and skirt. Pale red chalk illuminated her face and lithe body, her hair wound in plaits and tied together to form an elaborate tail.

Flutes and drums cut through the chatter of the onlookers. Young men with solemn faces acted as monitors, pacing up and down importantly in front of the dancers, making certain that ceremonial proprieties were followed during the Ngoma. The monitors carried tight bundles of sticks, which would soon be lit in the fires that the old women stoked. Any dancers who behaved improperly had the burning sticks hurled at them.

The Ngoma began, the dancers jumping up and down, their heads thrown back and their feet stamping to the music. Wamboi and the other Nditos, the maiden dancers, threw themselves forward on one foot and jumped back on their other foot, rocking with the motion. The young men, naked and virile, their hair elaborately maned, pigtailed and decorated with ostrich feathers, matched the girls' movements.

The rhythm of the drumming increased. Both maidens and warriors began walking sideways around the perimeter, their steps paced and dignified, their heads turned to the center of the ring.

The music quickened again. The dancers broke rank, Wamboi among them, jumping and running within the circle once more.

A clear voice rang out. A singer entered the circle, chanting an improvised ballad about the crested cranes. The hungry cranes desired the newly planted grain, and the farmers offered them one row to eat, if they would promise the rainfall. After the cranes feasted and flew away into the sky, the farmers replanted the row the cranes had eaten. Then the rain fell, nourishing the land, and made the harvest plentiful.

The singer walked in a long sliding step, imitating a crane, as the dancers chanted a chorus between each verse, praising both the crested cranes and the farmers. The song ended, Wamboi and the other Nditos lifting their voices in exuberant shrill shrieks.

Suddenly Kitau leapt high in the smoky light of the banked fires, landing near Wamboi. The other warriors encircled him, their spears swinging and jabbing the air. *Yes!* Wamboi thought, *the lion hunt!* She edged toward Kitau, her eyes flirting with him, his own flashing darkly back at her, their bodies half in the shadows, half in the glow from the freshly fed fires.

Kitau paused, and Wamboi placed her feet upon his feet, clasping her hands around his waist. Kitau slowly raised his arms and held his spear behind her in outstretched hands. He danced with Wamboi, who waited anxiously for him to lift his spear and strike the ground with it, signaling his desire for betrothal. *Yes, yes,* she thought. *Strike the ground behind me!*

She felt his arm muscles slide as he shifted the spear, his feet still dancing, her body riding along upon his. His spear struck the ground, and the monitors' burning sticks flew, striking her and Kitau. He shoved her away from him, brushing burning embers from his flesh.

The monitors surrounded her, dancing her away from Kitau to the edge of the circle and through it. Her uncle, Wanyangerri, pulled her roughly aside. "Come," he demanded. "You must not dance with Kitau again. Jogona Wamai has forbidden it."

* * * *

Center City Philadelphia, an autumn day in the last year of the 20th century.

Mariammo sat, enjoying her lunch in the Olde City Café, across from the two-story, pseudo-Colonial building where she worked as a secretary.

Olga, the cafe's owner, had tied the door open, allowing a cool breeze to enter, and now, a raucous banging.

Disturbed, Mariammo got up to check out the source of the noise. Looking out the door, she spied an elderly black man thumping on the mailbox at 2nd and Chestnut Streets.

She went in, finished her sandwich and coffee, then paid for her meal. The street drummer shrieked, then continued his irksome clanging.

Olga, at the cash register, was clearly upset by the racket. "Some people, they have to *play* at being exotic, you know!" she said, glancing pointedly toward the open doorway. "But not you," she added, her Ukrainian accent warming her words and her quick smile brightening her face. *"You are a real Kenyan!"*

Mariammo grinned. "Actually, my mother and I immigrated here to be with my Dad, an American, when I was three."

"You didn't have to study to be an American, like I did." Olga reminded her. "But you are beautiful, so I think you are a Kenyan princess!"

Mariammo blushed, pocketing her change. "Thanks. See you tomorrow."

Outside, the drummer shouted and let loose another barrage of clangs that competed with the whisk and rumble of traffic and the garble of pedestrian dialogue. The drummer elicited different timbres from the blue metal mailbox, his strange concert following her as she walked down the street, jarring her and yet mimicking something long-lost, perhaps hidden in her memory from her early Kenyan childhood.

* * * *

The next day, going to work, she stared at the mailbox. Just a mailbox. Not the drums of Africa calling her home.

She crossed the street cautiously, watching for traffic, then halted in mid-step.

The buildings, cars, and paved blacktop had vanished, replaced by a savannah stretching far into the distance. The drummer, now dressed in regal African splendor, stood within its lush grassland, his hand beckoning to her.

The chitter of insects, the trill of birds lulled her. Mariammo shut her eyes, sleep-heavy.

The blare of a horn startled her awake, her eyes blinking open to the chaos surrounding her on 2nd Street.

A car, its driver looking like a swallowed meal behind the windshield, occupied the spot where the drummer had—only seconds ago—stood.

The driver honked his car horn again impatiently, gesturing angrily at her. The car behind him shot out into the turning lane and sped past her. Other cars, bottlenecked at the intersection, honked at her. She rushed blindly onto the curb and the sidewalk and, heart pounding, hugged herself, frightened, having never before hallucinated in the midst of traffic in downtown Philadelphia.

She walked toward her office falteringly.

Bang-bang-bang-a-bang-a. Bang-bang-bang-a-bang-a.

Now the rhythm, the tonality of the drummer's handiwork upon the metal was flawless.

Calling.

Calling her.

Bang-bang-bang-a-bang-a. Bang-bang-bang-a-bang-a. BOOM! BOOM!

She turned to confront the man.

The drummer was nowhere in sight. A huge lion sprawled beside the mailbox, its yellow eyes inscrutable, boring directly into her own.

Other people walked by the lion without the slightest glance. Another hallucination!

Mariammo waited, determined to face the beast. Could an imaginary creature harm her?

The lion padded silently up to her, sat on its rump, and raised its magnificent head to lock eyes with Mariammo.

Feeling foolish, she spoke to it. "You can't be real."

A young couple, walking by, overheard her. The girl asked, "What's with *her?*"

"Crazy," her boyfriend decided. They continued on, laughing, not looking back.

"I've gone crazy," Mariammo told the lion.

"No," it answered, its voice low, nearly hoarse. "I have been sent to plead for your return. And to apologize."

"Apologize?"

"I caused your death, long ago. Beasts do not think, nor do they speak, except when the great Danbhalah says they must. I apologize, for beasts live only in the moment and act according to their instinct with no thought to the future, to the consequences of satisfying that instinct."

"But I'm not dead."

"No," said the lion, "but you were." It shook its great mane. "Come home, Wamboi. Come home and heal the people and the land."

The lion faded before her.

Mariammo drew a ragged breath. An old man approached her. "Lady, you all right? You been standin' there mumblin' to yourself for ten minutes."

She stared at him, regaining control. "I'm fine. Thank you."

She walked slowly to work and, pleading illness, took a sick day and went back home.

At her apartment, Mariammo went into her bedroom, took off her office clothes and put on her robe. Her cat, Muffin, a black and white shorthair, followed, watching curiously with steady green eyes.

Mariammo sprawled across the bed. Muffin jumped onto it, rubbing against her and pawing her. Mariammo stroked him. "It's just not possible," she insisted to the cat. "Lions do not talk and vast savannahs do not suddenly replace city streets." She rolled over onto her back. The cat settled down, curling up and yawning.

"I need rest." Mariammo closed her eyes and slept.

* * * *

Wanyangerri had led her away from the dancers, to a secluded grove, where his sisters waited, looking sternly at her. They ignored the despair in Wamboi's eyes. "It is an honor to marry Ndwetti Wamai," said her mother.

And her aunt chided her: "He will be chieftain one day, foolish girl, when his father goes to join the ancestors."

"But I do not *love* him," Wamboi repeated.

"Your duty is to the clan," her uncle told her. "You are of age, and the bride price has been set, a high one, including many cattle. Jogona will pay it. Your mother and aunt would have told you this tomorrow. But now we must smooth the near insult you and Kitau may have brought to Jogona and his son. We announce your betrothal tonight."

"No," Wamboi moaned.

"Yes. Dance no more with Kitau. Ndwetti is to be your husband. Come."

They returned to the Ngoma, her uncle drawing her to Ndwetti Wamai's side. The gangling youth with his long jaw and thin lips smiled at her as she approached him. Wanyangerri raised his hand high for silence. The fluting and drumming slowed to a halt, the chattering of the people died into a hum.

Her uncle placed her hand into Ndwetti's outstretched one as Jogona Wamai entered the circle in full ceremonial garb. The chieftain stood behind Ndwetti and Wamboi, placed one hand on her head and his other hand on Ndwetti's, and spoke clearly to his people: "My son and Wamboi are betrothed. This pleases me, and I will send them good magic that they may prosper and have strong sons and daughters. At the next full moon, they shall marry, and we will feast and dance again."

A loud murmur of approval swept through the crowd. Wamboi looked anxiously for Kitau. She found him; he stared sullenly at her. Wamboi looked away, her hand limp in Ndwetti's, hating his touch. But to disobey an elder would earn a harsh beating. To disobey their Chieftain—no one would dare.

The Ngoma resumed, an aura of celebration permeating it. Wamboi danced herself into a sweat, purging her anger and sorrow, moving away from Ndwetti. But he followed her, dancing beside and in front of her, holding out his arms, his spear within one hand, beckoning her to finish with *him* what she had earlier attempted with Kitau.

All eyes were on them. Wamboi, unable to rebel under the clan's open gaze, placed her feet on Ndwetti's and her arms around his waist. She held her own hands clasped together tightly, so as not to fall off of his dancing body, her nails digging into her flesh for courage. Ndwetti placed his arms at each side of her head, his spear firmly held in his right hand. He struck the ground triumphantly, claiming her as his own. Her eyes met his, burning with desire and pride. Wamboi kept her own face rigid and unemotional, gazing at his slender muscled shoulder until he tired of carrying her small frame. She stepped off his feet. He led her from the circle for a cooling drink.

In the morning, he would come to her uncle's manyatta, to take her from her mother's hut and lead her to her new home within the manyatta of Jogona Wamai, to be part of his father's household.

But her heart knew only the pain of being forced away from Kitau. For was he not also about to declare his love for her? If she rebelled and broke custom, bringing disgrace on herself, perhaps Ndwetti would refuse her. He would not want a woman like that.

She would not do too terrible a thing, simply hide in the forest just before Ndwetti came for her. Then he would know she was a difficult woman and declare her unworthy to be his bride. Her uncle would beat her, but she would heal. In time, the clan would forget, perhaps forgive her willfulness. And Kitau would wait for her, and perhaps at the next Ngoma, the old women would nod their heads and say that some things were meant to come to pass.

* * * *

The cool mist of early dawn had cleared. The woods at mid-morning echoed with myriad calls: monkey chatter, insect shrill, bird caws. Somewhere in the distance, water rushed and gurgled faintly. An elephant trumpeted, a bull, perhaps herd leader, calling to his cows and calves.

Wamboi grasped a thick lower branch and hoisted herself up the tree. She climbed higher, her skin beaded with sweat from the exertion. Her gathering pouch, heavy with berries, swung from her neck and shoulder, a feeble excuse for her absence.

From her perch in the tree, she spied the village far away and realized she had wandered to the boundary between forest and savannah, its open plains filled with many predators. She judged the quickest path back to her village and, glancing down to gauge her footing, descended to the ground. She began walking briskly away from the savannah.

And saw the lion, padding lazily toward her. It sprawled beneath a nearby tree, yawning at her, its forepaws stretching languidly, almost playfully, scratching on a tree root.

"Go away, friend lion," Wamboi said, using soft magic in her voice to ward the lion off. "Go back to the savannah from which you have strayed. The gnu herd awaits your chase. You do not wish me for your morning meal, for I am too thin and scrawny. Go find a fat gnu."

The lion jerked his head sideways and, for an instance, Wamboi thought her magic had worked. Then the big cat padded backwards and bent into a half crouch.

Wamboi turned and ran in a futile attempt to escape.

The leaves and twigs carpeting the forest floor crackled and rustled as the lion sprang after her.

She mumbled fervent prayers to the gods as she hooked her hands and arms around a sturdy tree limb, her muscles flexing to swing up to safety.

The lion's jaws clamped onto her leg, dangling a second too long. She felt its sharp teeth sink into her flesh and break the bone within. Pain, fear and the shock of blood loss sent her to her ancestors long before the lion finished eating.

* * * *

Mariammo awoke with an outcry, not yet freed from the horror of her dream, from the rake and plunge of the lion's claws and teeth. Laying very still, she stared at her bedroom ceiling. Slowly, thankfully, the sensation of pain and blind fear lessened and finally faded.

She rose stiffly from the bed and tremulously, irrationally, approached her full-length mirror. Slipping off her robe, she examined her body, but found nothing wrong. She rewrapped the robe around herself. She was going nuts, seeing the impossible, dreaming of this other woman, Wamboi, of her death, life and ardor for the handsome Kitau, and of her rigid uncle, Wanyangerri.

Muffin stretched, jumped lazily from the bed, and trotted through the hallway to the kitchen. Mariammo followed her, shuddering as the cat's teeth sharply crunched on its dry food.

Mariammo picked up her phone, dialing her family doctor, telling the receptionist that she had an emergency. Dr. Westerov picked up a minute later. Mariammo related her sudden onset of hallucinations and the death dream. An hour later, she sat in his office, being examined and tested for possible neurological trauma.

"On the surface, I can't find anything physically wrong with you," Dr. Westerov said. "I'll know more when the test results come back. Your problem may be physiological or psychological or a combination of both. But your straight-forward account of what happened, your having no history of psychosis, and the fact that you recognized the lion and savannah as hallucinations, despite your fear, shows you know the difference between fantasy and reality. I want you to take a mild tranquilizer I'm going to give you. And call me *immediately* if you have another hallucination. If I'm not here, have my service page me, night or day. Otherwise, I'll see you next week."

Mariammo thanked him, paid the receptionist and made a follow-up appointment. Back home, she drew a hot bath and relaxed. Later, the calmative working, she rested in bed, thinking of her life as an American woman, comfortable, safe and snug. She remembered her refusal to join her parents in their missionary work in Rwanda, her grief and guilt when they died in the Hutu uprising, staying with the beleaguered Tutsis while other

U.S. citizens evacuated the country, leaving Mariammo orphaned at the age of 22. With Muffin snuggling beside her, she finally cried out her tension and fell into a dreamless sleep.

* * * *

In the morning, she returned to her job, assuring her co-workers that she felt much better, and spent the day finishing yesterday's workload.

The day passed peacefully. She clocked out at five, tugging her coat around her as she left, a cold wind blowing off the harbor at Penn's Landing. She walked to the corner to head up 2nd Street and catch the El train home.

The drummer stood by the mailbox in his homeless tatters, oblivious to the cold. One of his hands rested quietly on the blue metal; with his other, he beckoned to her, almost coyly.

Mariammo steeled herself and walked up to him.

"I need to make sure you *are* real," she said. "Just a man standing on a corner. No drum, no savannah, no lion."

The man replied softly in a strange language.

"I don't understand, but it doesn't matter. I'm sure you can't understand me either. Look." She fumbled in her handbag and pulled out a dollar. "Here. It's cold out. Get yourself something warm to drink."

His hand, reaching out to take it, closed over hers. Mariammo tried to pull away. The drummer held on tightly, speaking in a rapid sing-song voice, his words incomprehensible.

She brought her free hand up, pushing against his iron grip, only to have him grasp it as well.

He said, "You were Wamboi, and you were lost to us, both by your disobedience and the lion who ate you."

Mariammo stopped struggling and stared at him. His language, while still foreign, had suddenly become clear, easily translated.

"My son would not marry another, when the mourning time had passed. I beat him, but still he mourned for you. My son angered the gods and brought bad luck. No rains came to nourish the grain and feed the cattle. Plants shriveled, hunting proved poor, animals sickened and died. The clan weakened, scattering and dying, as it moved in search of a better land. But the drought and famine moved more swiftly than we did. We came into Masai territory, and our tribes fought. And I, too, died, but as I died, I prayed to Danbhalah, the greatest of the gods, that one day my spirit would find you and ask you to return back to the time before your own death, to be a dutiful daughter to us all and undo the time of sorrow that destroyed us."

"But..." She struggled at first to answer in his unfamiliar language, then the words came fluently, as if she had always spoken them. "But the famine—your clan's destruction—would have happened anyway. What's done can't be undone!"

"Then our people will be no more. As I beat Ndwetti, he cursed us, that we would not let him mourn in peace. He prayed that we would suffer and die, as you had, and as he, too, would, without you. I told him that you had rejected him, that only a fool grieves for a woman who denied him her love. But he would not stop his grieving. He ranted at us and called us cold and unfeeling. He refused nourishment and weakened and died. And the land withered and died."

Mariammo fought against the drummer's grasp, reverting to English. "No. No! This is the twentieth century. You speak of the past, but it's gone." She shut her eyes. "I'm going to scream for help if you don't release me. I've hallucinated all of this. I refuse to believe it."

"Then open your eyes, Wamboi, betrothed of Ndwetti."

She lifted her lids reluctantly to stare at the drummer's elaborate attire and headdress.

"Danbhalah answered me, Wamboi. He wishes you to undo the time of sorrow."

A huge drum stood where the mailbox had been. Around them, the city had completely vanished, replaced by the rich seductive scenery and whispering sounds of lush African veldt and forest.

He released her hands. "Look upon yourself, Wamboi."

Her limbs and torso, smooth and dark, were draped with a long leather skirt and halter, beaded with bright swirling colors and patterns. Her arms and feet were bare, save for beaded anklets and bracelets. She felt her hair and brought a long ebony strand, twined with beads, before her eyes.

The drummer smiled at her, nodding, then lightly lifted her chin, causing her to gaze upward at his face. "Do you recall my name, Wamboi?"

"Jogona Wamai," she said.

"Yes. Your chieftain and father of your betrothed." He paused and breathed a long and tired sigh. "I cannot force you, Wamboi, to stay and marry him. To save him, and through him, our people. Stay for one month, one turning of our moon. Greet Ndwetti and your uncle Wanyangerri. No time will pass in your modern life, and I will return you to it, if you choose to leave us."

"If I did stay, and died from some other cause, would your son grieve and curse your people again?"

"It was not only love, but pride and unspent passion that caused both Ndwetti's and your own rebellion. Marriage calms such heated youth." He gently rubbed the huge drum beside him. Stretched and tightly bound, its covering displayed a tawny yellow fur. "The lion himself offered sacrifice to bring you back. He, too, died in the days of drought and famine, and his family with him. Instinct was not enough to save him. We must give thought to the needs of others. Decisions today change our world tomorrow, Wamboi."

"Wamboi." She tasted the name.

"It is who you once were and will be again if you choose to stay."

He extended his hand. She took it.

They traveled through the forest to the clearing that defined the western boundary of the Lumbwa village. The clan awaited her, their faces both curious and anxious. The din of their voices rose in a babble, then dropped to an abrupt hush.

A tall older man with grave eyes came forward and clasped her hands in his. Wanyangerri.

"Uncle," she said. He stood rock still, then his tear-swollen eyes released their burden, trailing pathways down his dusky cheeks. Wanyangerri hugged her fiercely, then released her.

In the crowd about them, she saw Kitau, his expression stiff. Perhaps he had grieved for her, too. She smiled at him sadly.

Ndwetti Wamai approached her hesitantly. She smiled at him as well. He threw his head back and let loose a trill of relief and hope. She couldn't help but laugh at his comical display of affection and yet it was also endearing.

* * * *

When Mariammo missed her appointment, Dr. Westerov phoned her apartment. No one answered. He called Mariammo's office and was told that she'd been missing from work for a week. When she hadn't called in nor returned her co-workers' calls by the third day of her absence, they had called the police.

The Philadelphia Police investigated. Mariammo had been seen once. She had asked a neighbor to adopt Muffin, pleading a lengthy family emergency overseas. The neighbor took the cat in, but Mariammo's apartment showed no further evidence that she'd ever left it, other than a cryptic message in an unknown tongue which she recorded on her answering machine tape.

Linguists at the University of Pennsylvania translated it, the language belonging to the Lumbwa, an African clan from Western Kenya. It no longer existed as it once was. Its remnants were called the Kipsogi. The message on the tape made no sense to the police: "I am Mariammo. I am also Wamboi. I have gone home."

DARIUS

Dedicated to the Family of Darius Meaux:
his mother, Vendetta; his father, Morrison;
and his brothers and sisters.

When my baby died, he was thirteen, locked in a body doctors once said would never see a second year of life. All of my other children, born before Darius and after him, were healthy kids. Darius was survived by his older sister, two older brothers, three younger sisters, and his father and me. Little Tamashi, our youngest, knew in her toddler mind that something sad had afflicted the family, but at three, she didn't understand, and maybe that was good. Because of our strong faith, she knew Darius went to God and heaven.

That would be all I would know, too, and it would have been enough, but a second gift occurred, the type that lifts the last remaining pangs of grief from your heart and turns them to gladness beyond human doubt.

A stranger who never said his name or asked for my thanks for it gave me that gift. That it came in a dream makes no difference. It was real.

Months before Darius died, a friend, Maggie, who works in my office, gave me children's books to read to Darius, Godzilla books done up not to frighten kids, with all the creatures from Monster Island. Nice creatures. They looked scary, but they weren't.

Darius couldn't read. He couldn't do much at all. We'd move him from bed to wheelchair, getting through each day, watching over him. We had to watch over him. He couldn't eat or drink. We fed him through a gastrostomy tube. His medicine often had to be changed, because it put him into a dead sleep, yet they prescribed it to stop the seizures he had.

His lungs…had a deformity. Sometimes he couldn't breathe. Always before, we caught this before it got worse, rushing Darius to the hospital. Then one night, he died in his sleep.

At the time, I was angry with God. I had just spent weeks worrying about more surgery the doctors were planning for Darius. His body was beginning to curl with cerebral palsy. But now I know it was his time to go to God; otherwise, we would have heard something.

Many of my co-workers came to the funeral parlor to pay their respects. A few had seen Darius those few times my family had brought him to my office, curled up and bundled in his wheelchair, trying to understand the sea of faces smiling at him. Maggie had never seen him, had probably pictured him as the average, physically handicapped child with a learning disability. She approached him in his coffin with the other people from work. I could see her face, the shock registering on it.

I've seen it all my life. His undersized, shortened left leg and small, babylike hands and arms never grew to normal size. The left and right sides of his skull were microcephalic, sunken in, not whole, since he came into this world. Handicapped. Learning disabled. Words. Yet his brown eyes would light up with the singing of the hymns, and he'd smile; I called it his *debonair* smile. He loved hearing our voices, the sound of the church organ. Small pleasures for a child who never knew the richness of this world.

Darius's appearance threw Maggie off, although I saw her look at his face and smile sadly, as if she, too, believed my son was truly now released from the limits of his life. She turned away and continued walking with the others, back to her seat.

But our good friend Nan stopped playing the organ and pointed me out to Maggie, though I was seated right in front, and Maggie almost passed by me and my husband and other children. Overwhelmed. That's what Maggie felt; it showed in her eyes. She reached out her hand, and I clasped it in mine, drawing strength from compassion. One quick moment of touch, conveying all it needs to, fortifying us.

It was weeks after his funeral that I was able to clean up his room, fix it up. And I found the Godzilla books, and sat in the chair near his bed, turning the pages of colorful illustrations, remembering my son's delight in them.

I was tired. You get tired, grieving, even when the worst of it is over. That's when I fell asleep, and that's when the dream came.

At first I was in this really nice, old-fashioned office, all wood-paneled, and when I looked around, this tall man was there, dressed just as old-fashioned, with a white, long-sleeved shirt with the sleeves rolled up and the collar unbuttoned, a gold-colored vest with a chain, light brown trousers and brown boots. His hair on his nearly bald head stuck up from the sides like wings framing his face. He wore little round glasses on his pointy nose, what they used to call spectacles, that had no side wires. His mouth was small like a cupid's, and his bright blue eyes smiled more than his mouth. Friendly eyes.

He didn't say anything at first, and I wasn't sure what to say to him, so I just smiled back. Then I saw that he held two thin books in his hands. The Godzilla books.

He saw me staring at them and clasped them together. "I was about to return them to the library," he said. "You're the mother of Darius."

"Yes."

"Well, he appreciated the humor in these books." Now the man smiled fully, lips and eyes. "And the love and care his family gave him." Tears formed in my eyes, and he caught it, quick as a cat. "There's no need to cry, missus. Darius is fine. If it's missing him, you are, well, he's waiting to see you. Just a visit, mind you. You're here on a special entry pass."

"Are you an angel?" I asked.

He hesitated, then said, "Of a sort."

I didn't question him further; he said he was taking me to Darius. I didn't want to mess anything up.

"Why don't you follow me to the library, and then we'll go outside?"

We went down a corridor and came to a hall filled with readers and books as far as I could see in every direction. Huge. There were tables and chairs and circular desks, I guess for checking the books out and in. He walked up to one of the desks and handed the librarian attending it the Godzilla books. She didn't stamp them or scan them with a machine. She opened them to their back inner pages, and my guide pressed his right palm to each. That done, he turned back to me and held out his hand.

I took it, wondering at his solid warmth. "This is heaven, isn't it?"

"A part of it," he said and led me down new corridors until he came to a side door and opened it.

We went outside. Neat concrete walkways and flower gardens were all around us. Not a scrap of litter anywhere. People sat on benches, on the grass, beside the flowers, reading, resting, talking. Far in the distance, I could see a street, but no cars, and there was no city noise. I looked around anxiously for my heart's desire.

"Over there," the angel man said, pointing to the right to a wide concrete patio that paralleled the library building. And to Darius.

He stood straddling a shining, silver, two-wheeler bicycle, both feet firmly and equally on the pavement, both arms fully extended, his hands grasping the handle bars. He was dressed in jeans, a white tee shirt and a green jacket, his feet in sneakers, and a baseball cap turned sideways, snug on his head, covered up most of his curly, black hair. "Look, Mom!" he shouted, the first time he ever spoke clear words, and his foot pushed down on the pedal. He rode over to me, stopped, steadied the bicycle, lowered the kickstand and got off, standing there quietly.

He was slightly taller than me now, maybe the normal height for a boy of thirteen. If things had been different for him on Earth.

"Darius," I said and this time didn't stop the tears welling up and streaking my cheeks. "You okay, Darius?" The man with the white wing-tipped hair and blue eyes patted my shoulder.

"I'm healed, Momma."

"You're…you're happy?"

"I'm not alone, Mom. I got friends. And…and love up here. But I miss you and the family. I'm watching over you, all of you. I'm watching over you now."

"Oh, baby." The tears were nearly choking my words. "Give me a hug. You can give me a hug now."

And he reached out and put his arms around me. "I can reach now. I can reach you, Mom." We stood there like that, our arms wrapped around each other, and Darius said, "All the time I was locked in that body, your love gave me courage to keep going on, but the one silly thing I remember was seeing a kid on a bicycle on TV, riding, flying down a road, and I always wanted to be like that. Like that kid. And when I got up here, the first thing they did was give me a bicycle. And I didn't understand until I realized I was whole. And that I could ride that bicycle. And I did. Flying with the wind of heaven in my hair."

He slowly let go of me. I let him, but as he released me, he gently, awkwardly, kissed my cheek. "You can't stay here long, Mom. You got other people needing you. But I want you to ride bikes with me before you go." He stood back, and I saw two bicycles stood where before there was only one. Mine had gold and red tassels and a golden frame.

"Darius…I don't know. It's been a long time."

"Come on, Mom. You can do it."

I looked at the blue-eyed man. He smiled, his mouth crinkling his cheeks. "You won't fall," he said.

"Oh." I laughed. "Okay."

Darius got on his silver bike, eager. I got on mine, getting reacquainted with the sensation, trying to remember my own childhood, when I'd go zipping off, wheels catching speed. "You don't have any tassels, Darius."

"It's okay, Mom. Tassels are for girls. Ready?"

"Ready!"

We pushed off on the pedals, and suddenly the library was gone, and we bicycled through a green field dotted with summer flowers.

"Faster, Mom, faster!" He sped ahead of me.

I felt youthful, playful. "I'm gonna catch you!" I shouted after him, laughing, and I did, and we flew over the grass and the flowers, the sun shining around us, side by side in a perfect day.

"I love you, Mom!" Darius shouted back against the wind as I seemed to ride into a great golden light and woke up.

I told my family about the dream, and they knew it was a gift. And I told Nan, and I told Maggie.

Maggie listened, and tears came to her eyes, but she didn't wipe them away.

"I'm going to write it down, tell it like a story, so I'll never forget every little part," I told her. "The angel man, the huge library, Darius and me riding through that beautiful field, free as two birds in the wind."

Maggie smiled, then laughed. "Just don't end it: 'And then I woke up.'"

"Why not?" I asked her gently, grinning a little. "That's how it ended. I woke up. Cause Darius wanted me to remember it until we ride those bicycles together again. And everyone knows you remember dreams best if you wake up right after dreaming. Except it wasn't a dream," I told her. "It was real. Darius woke up from the dream of mortal life, and he remembered us, he remembered us all. And he wanted me to see him, so I'd know."

"Know what?" she asked me.

"That the story isn't over."

GEORGE HARRISON, HERE

For those who like details, I died on November 29, 2001, lung cancer from smoking which I publicly blamed for that misfortune, and my ashes were placed in the Ganges and Yamuna rivers in India. Private ceremony, Hindu tradition. I watched them being scattered by family and friends. On the liner notes of my final album, *Brainwashed,* is a quote from the *Bhagavad Gita*: "There was never a time when you and I did not exist. Nor will there be any future when we shall cease to be."

I remember trying to get my head into the best meditative peace during my final days to effect the smoothest transition into *samsara,* whether rebirth occurred immediately or my *atman* transferred to a new existence in another realm. Ultimately we want to become one with *Brahman,* the one god who also exists in many other godly forms for Hindus, by achieving *moksha* through karmic learning. You don't have to understand these Hindu words, though you may want to explore them for your own spiritual learning. What I'm trying to say is that I found myself transitioning into another dimension initially following my death. I regained consciousness in a comfortable bed in a serene room filled with a myriad of plants. John sat beside the bed and smiled wistfully when my eyes opened to this new life, saying "Welcome home, mate."

"Where is home?" I asked, still groggy from crossing over.

"The astral, the upper, the higher planes, the afterlife, whatever you want to call it."

I sat up slowly. "Whatever they call heaven?"

John smirked. "Many I'm told are eternally vexed that no one can claim it or control it for one belief or another." He leaned over and grinned. "It's open to all, no matter what club you're affiliated with."

I fell back onto the pillow. "Do fights break out?"

"None that can hurt anybody. Generally puts a real fast damper on any squabbles."

"Bet you're glad somebody somewhere finally is giving peace a chance."

"Yeah, the Lennon manifesto finally found a home. Just not on Earth. So are you up to a tour of your new peaceful neighborhood, George Harrison?"

I sat up again, flexing my muscles, rubbing my neck. Everything worked but my body felt strange. I stood up, pulling off the bed covers, and found I was dressed in blue jeans, a white t-shirt and was barefoot. My psyche felt dizzy and I took a calming breath, but it felt strange, like inhaling and exhaling were difficult.

"We breathe differently in these bods," John said. He held up a pair of sandals. "Here. A present."

They fit my feet. I noticed he was wearing his favorite color: white. White shirt, jacket and trousers, white sneakers on his feet. He was clean-shaven, his brown hair shoulder length and neat with moderate fringe brushing about his forehead and ears. I noticed my own hair was also still neatly Beatlesque and my face smooth. "Actually, John, I'd like to see how my survivors are getting on."

"Okay." He linked his right arm with my left. "Who'd ya want to see first?"

"Olivia and Dhani."

"It's helpful if you travel with your eyes shut, George. Just think about going to wherever they are. You'll know when you've arrived. Oh, and yeah, we'll be invisible if we're in the mortal world."

"Okay." I closed my eyes and thought of my wife and son. A second later, I felt their presence and looked to see. We were on the banks of the Ganges and my ashes were being strewn. We stayed for the ceremony and I tried to speak to Olivia and Dhani but they didn't react, except for when John and I finally turned to leave and I looked back. Dhani had turned to stare in my direction, his face reflective, as if he sought some truth. I smiled at him as John linked my arm again and we went back to the spiritual plane. My eyes weren't closed and I saw the vast array of rainbow colors streaking all about us as we traveled there.

* * * *

"Ringo came to see me, you know," I told John. "In July, while I was in the hospital in Switzerland, but he couldn't stay. His daughter was having surgery in Boston. I asked if he wanted me to come with him. That got a laugh out of him. Then on November 12th I was in New York City for radiotherapy and he and Paul and I got together. Our last time. Then I went to L.A. and died on the 29th. That's all I remember until I woke up here."

John nodded. "They asked me to greet you first. You'll be called to do what passes for orientation here, get you a place to call your own, reunite you with any deceased family and friends you want to meet up with. Stu's still up here if you want to get together with him later. Then you'll get your own handbook of rules, which are thankfully not too many, with places of interest and activities to suit you, now that you've got eternal time on your hands, unless you get called upon to reincarnate."

"Sounds a bit departmental. What do we do to have a bit of fun around here? Providing it's allowed."

John looked at me slyly. "We could go down and haunt Paul a bit. Both he and Ringo generally know it's me, pulling their mortal chains. I also did some earthly excursions just to tease people, especially the ones who think they're contacting the dead and charging other fools or paying charlatans big bucks for it. Give them all the wrong answers."

I raised my brows. "Did you try to haunt me?"

"I looked in on you, me lad, but I didn't play games. Watched over you, especially when that maniac nearly killed you at home and Olivia smashed him. It wasn't easy for you since. I watched over you, mate."

I nodded. "Glad to hear it. I wouldn't mind playing a trick or two on Paul."

John grinned. "I like moving things around a bit. Like he knows exactly where something was and then it's not and he can't find it and gives up. Then an hour later, he finds it exactly where it originally was. And he says, out loud mind you, 'I know it's you, John. Why don't you do something useful and help me write some good lyrics for that new song I'm working on?'"

"Do you?"

John nodded. "Yeah, sometimes I do. He was our mate; we all had a special bond."

I nodded back. "I wouldn't mind visiting Ringo, too."

"I don't tease him so much. Sometimes just flicker the lights."

* * * *

We didn't really play parlor tricks, which are passé now. No table-rapping among the intelligentsia. I also learned that the Powers That Be don't promote idleness in the afterlife. John had been up here since December 9, 1980 and being the type of bloke who wanted to accomplish goals in his life, whether mortal or beyond, he'd been trained to be a spiritual guide in the early '80s and had ten charges he watched over in their earthly lives. I had been one of them. He was fond of the remaining nine, some more than others, especially if they didn't have the advantages of the Beatles and their famous colleagues but still made the best of their lives, creatively and spiritually.

One of them was a woman eight years his junior named Lila. When John died, the grief felt by his fans around the world overwhelmed him. When everyone meditated over or prayed for him during the moment of silence called for on most of the radio stations shortly afterwards, Lila's intense heartbreak drew him to her. He traveled through the astral byways to her small apartment and discovered she was strongly but privately psychic. When John arrived in her kitchen, she was crying and backed up in surprise, capable of seeing him but couldn't stop her tears. John told me he spoke firmly to her: "None of that now! We'll have none of that!" And he hugged her and later became her guide. They had a lot in common and were drawn to each other, but any love between them had to be platonic due to rules up here.

Over many a pint of astral beer or the various happy hour beverages they serve in the upside pubs, John told me of one major dispute he and Lila had which nearly ended their long-distance friendship. She was extremely critical of some of his former activities to promote world peace.

"She lived through the sixties, seventies and eighties, and had her own hopes for saving the world from human foolishness. And she loved the Beatles ever since she saw us on the Sullivan show in 1964, though she wasn't exactly a Beatlemaniac, just loved our music and our happy-go-lucky attitudes. I was her favorite but then I changed with the Vietnam War and the politics and the furious backlash over my remark about Jesus not being as popular as the Beatles. Not that she cared about that since she was Jewish and reform at that. What turned her off wasn't my shouting about peace. It was what I was and wasn't doing to change the world and end war. She was practical and I was, according to her, only interested in symbols without solid methods to make my goals a reality."

I hesitated. "I questioned some of your behavior about that, but decided to keep the peace between us," I quipped.

He snorted. "I'm sure it wasn't just me you questioned."

I leaned back and took a swallow of my happy juice. "I never come between a man and his major influence, if I can avoid it."

"Yeah, yeah. I know what influence you're talking about."

"And we can relegate that to your past now. So what did little Lila razz you so badly about?"

"She started with my lounging in pajamas in the Amsterdam hotel bed in 1969 to promote peace. Said it was a useless gesture, did nothing at all to cure the real causes of war. I pointed out that at the second Bed-In for Peace in Montreal a couple of months later, I wrote the song, 'Give Peace a Chance' and it became an anthem against the Vietnam War, and Yoko and I had billboards around the world shouting 'War is Over! If you want it.' Lila said the billboards were a waste of money, preaching mostly to those already converted, still not healing the real causes of war like famine and illness and bigotry. I pointed out that we gave to charities and peace activists and she was mostly all right with that. But when I said that fighting for peace often put the activists in the line of fire by the power mongers who didn't want peace, she questioned the motives and behavior of some of those activists. The same old crap. She wanted a perfect solution with no ambiguity. I told her she was a dreamer like me but didn't want to pay the price for making the dream come true."

"What did she say to that?"

"She backed off a bit, said that it was no solution to fight violence with reverse anger and bullying. She also didn't like the acorn planting as a symbol. Said all talk and no plan to help humanity overcome the world's real sorrows equaled failure."

"I have to agree with her, John. That's why we had the concert for Bangladesh. So what did *she* do to ease the world's pain?"

He gave a small laugh of concession. "She gave whenever she could to charities, considering her budget. Still does. Wrote letters to the editors, poems of hope and peace. She also razzed me for being what she called belligerent and rude in my activist days." He grinned. "Lila could be bitchy herself, but I knew her heart was in the right place. I swallowed my anger and asked what she thought of 'Imagine.' She loved that song and proved it by getting involved with the local peace movement during the Gulf War and sang it at a rally."

"So you resolved your dispute?"

"She agreed to a truce when I agreed I could have done more to promote beneficial cures for the causes of war, conceding that point to her. She forgave me for my wicked tongue and now I'm helping her write a peace plan for curing all the ills of humankind."

I couldn't resist a small smile and laugh. "Is it any good?"

John shrugged. "I'll let you know if she finishes it, George."

* * * *

I've been here now for nearly a score of years by mortal standards. Time moves about three times more slowly here, plenty enough to learn, create and share with others living the high life. I haven't been called to reincarnate nor asked for it. Too much I want to do, you know. We interact with those still mortal, transferring ideas born upside in every human field to be utilized by humanity on Earth. It's a lovely afterlife. And we have music. Lots and lots of music. John introduced me to many legends now singing and playing in the dimensional venues here. He and I continue to use our talents to promote our own hope for healing the strife still plaguing our brothers and sisters below.

Got to go in a few minutes. John and I are part of a major show in the Elvis Amphitheater. We have a great line-up of performers who've joined our population over the years. Blues, pop, rock, folk in our sphere of concerts. John's written a new peace song about seeking those *practical* solutions, and I've got a new one about discovering your inner peace to heal the turmoil of your heart. We haven't forgotten you people still struggling and hoping on that third planet from the sun in the Milky Way galaxy not so far away from us.

Ta-ta, luvs.

THE GIFT

I have been an unofficial elf most of my life, helping people quietly whenever they came across my path. I also hope to help others...some-how...through my writing, but on that early evening one December, my elven gifts were the ones apparently being called on.

Initially I had no more intention to intervene than anyone else on the train platform. He stood near the exit steps of the elevated train in the Frankford section of Northeast Philadelphia. He had the prerequisite ruddy jowls, cascading white curly hair reaching to his shoulders and covering his lower face and chest in a sumptuous beard. His Santa suit looked authentic, and I smiled as he got off the El two cars down from mine with other rush hour travelers.

I headed for the exit still smiling when the jolly old geezer approached one passenger then another as they hurried past, avoiding him as he called out: "Excuse me? Could you help me?"

Flurries of booted feet, hunched overcoats and tightly clutched hand-bags. He delayed a man in a long grey woolen coat.

"Excuse me, sir? Won't you please help me?"

The man laughed, heading down exit steps, throwing "Go home, Pops. You're drunk!" over his shoulder.

The old fellow stood on the platform, perplexed and appearing indig-nant at the man's remark. People jostled by him. He held up his arms in a plea. "Please. I'm trying to get home. Won't somebody help me?"

I watched the faces of the other travelers. Some were averted, some smiled, others grinned wildly. But they all drifted down the stairs.

I found I couldn't desert him. It may be a blessing or it may be stupid-ity, but I believe in magic. In magic in a material world.

I couldn't rid myself of the impish thought that this *was* Santa Claus. Saint Nicholas. Kris Kringle. That oversized employer of elves and rein-deer. Ho, Ho, Ho!

My elfish bent asserted itself. Reason flew off into the cold December sky.

"I'll help you," I called.

He turned his head and looked at me as if he recognized me, then walked over with a polite stately nod. "I thank you, young lady."

"You're welcome. What's the problem?"

"The problem, yes." He resumed nodding in the droll manner of one who's caused his own precarious situation. "Well, I seem to have been given some very wrong directions." He held up one white-gloved hand, first finger extended. "That's the first problem."

"Well, we can try to get you directions to wherever you're heading. But what else is wrong?"

A blush heightened his already rouge-tinged cheeks and forehead. "I'm afraid I'm temporarily embarrassed."

"Huh?"

"I've been robbed."

"That's terrible," I commiserated cautiously. "Did you tell a policeman?"

"Well, I'm afraid I hadn't realized it until…" He collected his thoughts. "You see, I was visiting Philadelphia, and having conducted my business here sought out a cab to drive me to the airport. But none of your cabs would stop." He shook his head. "Must be the suit. Doesn't inspire folk the way it used to, at least not before Christmas on a busy city street.

"I asked a passing gentleman how I might get to the airport and he directed me to your airport shuttle, an underground train that travels there. He instructed me to go to the subway at 15th and Market Streets and so I did.

"Once there, I asked a teller where I might board the train that ran to the airport. She asked me the direction I was heading for and I told her north."

"North… Well, you headed in the right direction. You mean Northeast Airport, right?"

"No, no. When I said north, I meant my flight destination. Which she apparently misunderstood. She pointed past the turnstile, telling me to take the stairs marked Frankford. I had misgivings about her advice but my attempt to voice them was met by a look of utter dismissal. The crowd behind me had become quite restless and so I clutched my knapsack and descended those stairs.

"The train came and the boarders swelled about, entering and exiting it. Not the nicest sort of train, doors snapping open and shut nastily. As I entered, I felt a bump and jostle at my side, and my knapsack was gone, no longer in my hand. The train doors had shut and, studying the floor and the surrounding area, I knew I had not dropped it in the rush. And as the train whistled through to the next stop, an elderly woman seated near me told me she had seen a young man rob me of it as he left the train."

I didn't respond immediately.

"I do apologize for keeping you here so long. But I am quite lost and this doesn't resemble an airport." He sighed. Santa Claus sighed.

"Well, where is your home?"

"The North Pole," he said with an absolutely straight face.

"The North Pole," I repeated with a smile that was more than slightly out of kilter.

"Yes, I go by way of Seattle, Washington with a stopover in Chicago. Or would if my return flight ticket hadn't been absconded off with…along with my other belongings."

He seemed both genuinely depressed and sincere, but just the same…

I grasped at the opener he'd given me. "What airline were you taking?"

"Northwest."

"That takes you to the North Pole, huh?"

"Yes, my dear young lady." He inclined his head in a nod; his eyes twinkled to match the affable smile he wore. "It travels to Alaska and then I have private transportation to carry me to destination's end."

"Well," I murmured, wariness showing, "I'm certain your flight's out of International Airport, well past Southwest Philadelphia in the opposite direction." We stood there, him without a spare nickel, me without a lot of spare cash to help him and wondering if I had any spare brains left in my head. "Perhaps we should find a policeman."

Santa shook his head. "He'd tell me to go down to the station house and report the crime. I don't think it would help."

"But they might drive you to the airport."

"Not likely. I'd say they have other things to do than provide transportation for lost travelers."

"Or direct you to a Traveler's Aid office."

"Now that's a possibility. I'm sure there's one at the airport. But I'd rather not report the crime." He saw my hesitancy. "It'd be bad publicity. What would the children think?"

An El train had pulled in, emptied, and was sitting, waiting for its return ride back to Center City. I fished in my shoulder-strap handbag and pulled ten dollars from my wallet. A sap is a sap. But, Lord, he *looked* like Santa Claus. "Here. Take this and take the train back to 15th Street. Don't bother with the Airport Shuttle. I don't know its schedule and I'm sure you want to get to the airport and the Traveler's Aid office as soon as possible. Go to The Bellevue Hotel at Broad and Walnut. I think they have an airport limousine and a nice lobby you can wait in until the limo's available."

"Are you sure they'll let anyone board it? Not just hotel guests?"

I wasn't sure. "I don't know. But I can't see why not."

He looked down at his red Christmas suit. A news headline flashed across my mind: VAGRANT SANTA ARRESTED AT THE BELLEVUE.

"You're right," I said, wincing. "The desk clerk might not believe your story."

"I know I'm imposing," he said, his voice gentle, "but you're the only one who's offered to help me. Do you think you might take me to the airport? I'll reimburse you for any costs as soon as I get home. You have my word on it!"

"I…umm…don't even know your name."

He hesitated slightly, then asked: "Do you want to know the truth, young lady?"

"Of course!"

"My name, then, is S. Claus. I am also known as Kris Kringle and as Jolly Old St. Nick, although that is largely due to a brother of mine who carries on the tradition in the Netherlands. The S. stands for Santa."

"It can't be," I mumbled, vowing silently to end all philanthropic ventures in my life from that moment on.

"You asked for the truth. Many things we think can't be, well, in fact, are. Look at me," he commanded. "Go on! Look at me closely…with your heart."

I studied his face, his eyes twinkling again. I saw stars in a night sky above new fallen snow on a Christmas Eve. I smelled sweet plum pudding and fresh evergreen boughs. I saw children, now young, now old, of many eras gone and here and yet to come dancing in his eyes. I saw their innocence and faith, as they drifted into sleep, their belief in this totally giving person. "Dear God! You're really him!"

He threw his head back at my look of astonishment to laugh heartily enough to satisfy the strictest traditionalist. "Yes, I'm Santa Claus. Oh," he laughed again, "does me good to laugh! Does me good to know someone has a little faith!"

I started to deny it, to run back to the sanctity of sanity.

"You're not going to lose it now, are you, Carol?" he admonished with a smile.

"How did you know my name?"

"I didn't until we connected…until you believed. After belief, it's a simple matter. I look into *your* heart."

"But…"

"Would you escort me to the airport? I would be so grateful. And I'll answer any questions you have while we journey back to 15th Street."

How a mythological figure could spring to life as I came home from work during the Christmas season was a mystery to me. But a writer's mind is always open, willing to test the water if a mystery might be solved, or at least have light shed upon it. I pulled a small writing pad and pen out of my handbag. "All right, Santa. There've been a few things I always wanted to ask you. It's getting cold and this train's leaving soon. Let's get on."

As we seated ourselves, the doors of the train slid together, shutting. It chugalugged back to Center City.

"I have a lot of questions," I began.

"Fine. But must we use that pen and paper? Couldn't you keep it up here?" He tapped his forehead. "It's so formal, I'd be watching my every word!"

"It's just for notes. Memory joggers."

He stayed silent.

I put away the pen and paper, grinning.

"Thank you. First question?"

"First question. If you're Santa Claus, how come people buy gifts?"

"Now, Carol." A patient smile developed on his lips.

"What's my last name?" I asked abruptly.

"Excuse me?" he blinked.

"My last name. You knew my first. What's my last name?"

He studied me for a minute. "Matthews. Carol Ann Matthews. And you always wanted a piano. Not from me; from your parents. You were too old to believe in me…at least that's what they told you."

My mouth hung open. "I still haven't gotten one."

He shrugged and gestured with his hands expansively. "I'm afraid you're on your own for this year, dear. My work quota's finished."

"Oh."

"Maybe next year." He smiled again. His eyes were placid pools. "I'll see what I can do."

The child in me, long buried, believed him. "Oh, well. If you could…"

"I'll give it my best effort. Now, you had questions?"

"Yes. I'll come back to that other one later. First off, what are you doing here in your Santa Claus suit when it's not Christmas Eve? Why didn't you take your sleigh and reindeer? Aren't you supposed to be a master of invisibility and all that?"

He held up his hand to stop the torrent. "First off, as you put it, I had the bad sense to schedule a business trip on the day Mrs. Claus does her laundry. When I looked for my good travel suit, I found it was at the cleaners and wouldn't be done until Tuesday. My other business suit had a rip in the seam…too many cookies, I'm afraid. Mrs. Claus hadn't had a chance to repair it, what with supervising the elves and feeding their little faces." He saw my incredulous look. "Yes, Carol. There *are* elves."

"Elves?" I held my jaw tightly. It threatened to expand.

"Little people with slightly pointed ears, if you prefer," he conciliated.

"Midgets?"

"Good Lord, no! They're not human. At least not Homo Sapiens. They're another species and not entirely visible by choice which accounts for your and society's amazement."

"Okay," I conceded. "So there really are elves…somewhere. Go back to your story. Your suit was at the cleaners…"

"Yes, my suit was at the cleaners and I had a trip scheduled to Philadelphia to buy a very rare book. A very special person had need of a volume of stories published in 1890. Out of print now. I had to get an original: it only had one printing."

"A kid wanted an old book for Christmas?"

"It wasn't for a child. It was for an adult."

"An adult. And you were going to sneak in and tuck it under his tree."

"Not at all. I was going to situate it in the right spot for his friend to buy it for him for the holidays."

"Huh?"

"My business operations aren't just confined to toy-making and sleigh rides once a year with magic reindeer."

"Oh. Business outlets."

"In a manner of speaking. Have you ever wondered how you managed to find the right gift for the right someone almost right away? A gift almost custom-made and always for someone deserving?"

"Yes...it's only the people I *have* to buy for that I have a hard time finding things. If it's someone I love, it almost pops into my hands."

"There you are. Mind you, don't spread this around. It's company information."

"Not a word. Go on, please."

"Thank you. Well, despite Mrs. Claus's misgivings, I decided to wear my Christmas suit, it being only a week or two from the holiday. There'd be many mock Santas on the streets, spreading the spirit of the season. For any questioners, I'd say I was going to or from a charity benefit. This suit brought a lot of smiles on the flight up. In fact, I was quite a hit with two children, Lucy and Daniel. Their parents have already received their presents and for the right price."

"You gave them a discounted price?"

"Someone has to keep inflation out of the toy market, and this year it's been a doozy!" He let out a guffaw.

A couple of smiles lit up the faces of the passengers in our car. We whistled underground to the 2nd Street stop.

A silence descended on us, then I said, "So you came to Philly, bought your book, and the rest is history."

"That about wraps it up."

"I'll help you," I promised.

"Thank you, Carol." He watched the doors slam shut at 2nd Street. "We're nearly there. Do you have any other questions?"

"Do you really go down chimneys and do reindeer really fly?"

"Now those are trade secrets."

"Magic."

"Magic; a bit of the myth, the mystique. But I will tell you—the real magic lives inside you." He leaned closer, emphatically. "Where you arrive, how you travel, it's really irrelevant. It's what you have to give when you get there that counts."

I nodded.

"Any other questions?"

"How old are you?" It popped out.

His eyes lit again with that twinkle; his ruddy mouth stretched into an impossible grin. "A rather rude question for anyone but Santa Claus, eh?"

"Oh...I'm sorry."

"No, no, no. It's quite all right." He thought of an answer, then gave it. "I'm old enough that you're all, each and every one of you, my special children."

We were at 13th Street.

"I have no further questions, your honor."

He reached over to pat my hand. "You're a good girl."

"I try." The train entered 15th Street. "This is our stop."

We got off and started toward the exit stairs. I glanced at the eastbound platform, amazed that just one hour ago I had left from there to go home from my workaday world. "Santa, wait." I strained my eyes. Across the tracks, what looked like a bag lay half-hidden under the opposite stairway. "What color was your knapsack?"

"Blue. Why?"

I pointed.

"Yes, I do believe that's it!"

"Come on. We can go through the overpass and get it."

I scurried up the stairs ahead of him, went through the passageway, and down the other side to retrieve the satchel for him.

It was missing the usual cash and credit cards but the book and his flight ticket were inside.

"What luck!" he said as I touched the book—of 19th Century French short stories—reverently, then checked his flight ticket.

"Look. Your flight's at eight o'clock. It's only 6:30. We can make it."

"If the airport limousine leaves on time."

"Come on," I said and led him out to the street and across it to an automatic bank teller. I punched in a withdrawal of $40.00.

"I believe that's your budget money," he said.

"I trust you." He said nothing, but smiled gratefully. "Come on, let's get a cab. This is your busy season, isn't it?"

"Absolutely."

A United Cab was parked in front of the Bellevue, its cabbie glad to have an airport fare. "Where ya goin', Santa? The North Pole?" he chuckled.

"Close enough," Santa answered with the customary wink.

The cab fare came to $25.00 with our generous tip. At the airport, Santa confirmed his flight at the Northwest desk and, with their help, made some phone calls about the missing credit cards. On one of those calls, a woman's voice chided him sharply. Mrs. Claus, I presume.

When his flight was called, we said good-bye in the departure area.

We shared a big hug, at first not speaking.

"I have your address. I'll reimburse you for the cab fare, Carol. Now you be careful going home."

"I will, Santa. Santa?"

"Yes?"

"Do you know what I want for Christmas?" My voice, I knew, sounded plaintive.

"Yes," he answered, "and you're going to get it."

A sigh escaped, from the depths where dreams wait. "I love you, Santa."

"I love you, too. And thank you for helping me. You know, that's the greatest gift you can give."

"Merry Christmas."

"Merry Christmas, Carol."

He turned to go. I watched him, a quiet man in a red suit with white fur trim, carrying a blue knapsack. As he entered the runway tunnel to his flight, he smiled and waved. I waved back.

I wondered what Santa thought I wanted for Christmas. When I'd asked him, I hadn't a blessed idea myself. Nothing material at least.

One week later, an envelope with no return address but postmarked "Anchorage, AK" and a package from California arrived in the mail. The package was from a well-known writer whom I admired and had written to a few weeks back, feeling discouraged and asking his advice. His reply lifted me back on my feet. I read his encouragement, feeling his presence, believing, caring. With the letter, he had sent a copy of his favorite book on writing. "Read it ten times," he wrote. "It should help you with some of your problems."

The envelope from Anchorage contained a Christmas card depicting Santa stuck inside a chimney, surrounded by puzzled reindeer.

I opened it to find a check for $25.00 from S. Claus. The printed text inside read: "I'm giving up cookies after Christmas…" Under it, in handwritten script, he had written: "Thank you, Carol, and have a joyous Christmas. Santa."

I framed the letter from my favorite author, put the card in my keepsake box, gave the book its first reading, and deposited the check.

I know there may be some diehard out there, demanding proof of the plum pudding.

All I can tell you as an unofficial elf is that I believe in Santa, in myself, and have hope for the future.

And that the check didn't bounce.

GOTTA DANCE

Valerie Robbins had once dreamt of becoming a professional dancer. She had the talent, but not the stamina or finances to support herself between casting calls. Now, at the slightly ripened age of 27, she danced in her apartment, creating her own impromptu choreography. And on one autumn evening, she was swirling by herself to *The Emperor Waltz* when a ghost suddenly appeared in her living room. Not just any ghost. A very famous one.

The tape continued to play on her stereo. Valerie couldn't quite catch her breath.

Fred Astaire grinned at her, leaning suavely against the archway.

"I'm dreaming," she told herself. "That's got to be it. I mean, it's 1997, and you're dead, and even if you weren't, what would Fred Astaire be doing in my apartment? So this is a dream, and I'll wake up in a minute, the way I always do when I realize I'm dreaming."

"No, you're not dreaming." His voice, light and lyrical, held that touch of panache she so admired in his musical comedies. He hesitated charmingly. "We're wasting some perfectly good dance music. Shall we?"

He moved to her side, placed one hand around her waist, and with his other reached for her hand. Val pulled away, frightened. "You're a ghost!"

He backed off. "But a rather solid one for now and perfectly harmless. Are you sure you don't want this dance? Well, if you don't mind, these feet never could resist a good tune."

He began waltzing around the room, using her couch and chairs for some of his rhythmic leaping steps, at one point knocking over her lamp, catching it, and righting it, all in one effortless and phenomenally graceful movement.

"Okay! Okay!" Val finally recovered both breath and tongue. "What are you doing here?"

"What am I doing here?" he said between steps. "Well, quite honestly, I've heard that you like dancing."

"Um, dead people generally don't materialize in my apartment for a dance."

The waltz ended, and Fred's impromptu performance finished with an unbroken movement, in which he folded his arms, then cupped his chin lightly. "You're right. There is another reason. But I thought a little tripping the light fantastic might, well, lighten it."

"Is it something bad?"

"Mmn…not too bad, if you don't let it be. It won't ruin your life, if you overcome it."

"What?!"

"Are you sure you won't have *one* lighthearted dance with me? After all, if this is a dream, you'll wake up and leave me with a broken heart."

The way he said that held the same timbre of longing he'd always used on Ginger Rogers in half-a-dozen movies. Ginger had always succumbed to him at that moment, dressed ravishingly in her silks, flounces and feathers, and so did Valerie, in her Loony Tunes tee shirt and blue jeans. He played the scene well, appearing instantly beside her again. This time she took his proffered left hand as his right slid around her waist.

He tilted his head toward the stereo. "Maestro, if you please." Valerie watched her stereo's buttons click by themselves, turning off the cassette deck and turning on the radio. The channel changer swept past several stations before resting on one. It began an old Beatles favorite of Val's: Paul McCartney's dulcet tones caressing "Till There Was You," arranged into a light, melodious cha-cha.

She was relieved when he didn't try for some intricate choreography. He stayed with simple steps, exerting gentle pressure on her lower back, leading her.

The song ended; the afterglow remained.

She curtsied coquettishly.

He bowed gallantly.

"So what is this major happening coming up in my life, Sir Ghost?"

"Aw!" He tsked. "I wish you wouldn't address me like that. And I'm, uh, not allowed to tell you."

His glib remark acted like an ice cube down her back, shocking her back into fear and denial. "I'm imagining you."

"No…" he started, but she cut him off.

"I've been working too hard, and this is the result. I'm going to clean up this place, and go to bed. In the morning you'll be gone, and I'll be sane again!"

When he didn't answer, she took that for proof of her returning rationality. She bustled around the apartment, cleaning up the dishes, setting out an outfit for work in the morning. She started undressing for her shower in the bedroom, with a curt, "Imaginary people had better not be here, or they'll be playing a new role: Peeping Tom with an imaginary black eye," when her cat, Harpo, strolled up to her and yowled. "Oh, God, I forgot your litter box." She lumbered in tee shirt and panties into the kitchen, grabbed a plastic bag, and scurried into the bathroom. Val took the pooper scooper and bent quickly to dump the litter box refuse into the bag.

When she straightened up, a fiery pain ripped down her back and through her left leg. "Oh, my God, what have I done now?"

She tried to ignore it, carrying the bag to the kitchen trash. She'd had aches and pains before, but they had always gone away. She drew a hot bath. It soothed the pain but not by much. Gritting her teeth, staying in the steamy water, she remembered the cryptic remark Fred Astaire—who had now disappeared as any proper hallucination ought to—had made: that something bad would happen.

The pain ran like lava down her back and leg. Val got out of the tub and dried off. She put on a granny gown, and set up her heating pad on her bed, positioning her left side slowly down on it. Pulling the covers over herself for warmth, praying for the throbbing agony to cease, she turned her head to the far wall. And began to pant, astonished, as Gene Kelly, arms folded sternly, stared grimly back at her.

"You're dead, too," she told him weakly.

He graced her with a small smile. "I know," he said, then shook his head. "I'm afraid heating pads and hot soaks aren't going to cut it. You'd better get dressed and call someone to take you to a hospital." He glanced at the clock on her dresser. "Too late to find a doctor's office open."

Val groaned. "I'm dying. You're here to take me to that dance hall in the sky."

He chuckled, softly, sympathetically. "Hardly. You've sprained your lower back and pinched your sciatic nerve. You need some anti-inflammatory and pain relief medicine. You won't get it lying there. Come on now. Get up and dress. Who can you call to take you to the local hospital?"

Val rose slowly, and with shaking hands, struggled back into her clothes. She pulled on her sneakers and took excruciating baby steps to the kitchen phone.

Her boyfriend Wayne lived in Paoli, nearly an hour's drive to her apartment in northeast Philadelphia. She couldn't wait that long. Michael, her friend and a medical intern, lived downstairs. She steadied her hand and dialed his number. He answered on the third ring.

"Hello?"

"Mike?" Val panted. "This is Valerie. I've hurt my back and I'm in a lot of pain. Can you come up? I may need to go to the hospital."

* * * *

The emergency room doctor unknowingly confirmed Gene's diagnosis, gave Val a temporary medicine supply and prescriptions, then discharged her. Then Michael drove her home and tucked her in as Val thanked him profusely. He left at one in the morning, insisting that she call him, if she needed anything.

Val rested fitfully, drowsing off and on, only to be awakened by murmuring voices.

She switched on her bedside lamp. Gene Kelly and Fred Astaire sat side-by-side on the edge of her bed, Fred lifting his hand against the glare from the lamp. "You really ought to get some more sleep," he said.

"I can't sleep. I'm hallucinating again!"

"She thinks we're figments of her imagination," Fred explained.

"Imagine that," Gene quipped, then added more soberly, "I really can't blame her."

"I'm also hurting again," Val moaned, and shifted her body, which didn't help at all.

"We can't make that sprain and nerve pinch go away," Gene said. "Not right away. But we can speed up the healing process."

"Is that why you're here? To heal me?"

"To help you heal," Gene agreed. "That's certainly on the agenda."

"We're here to make sure you don't stop dancing," Fred said, as if it were a command, not a challenge.

"Dancing," Val muttered.

"Yes," he said. "We have it on the best authority that as a result of this injury, you'll give up dancing, fearing you'll reinjure yourself. Of course, you'll also become miserable, withdrawn, and a hypochondriac. Your friends will try to cheer you, but you'll reject their gentle advice, becoming more lonely and self-destructive. And when you finally manage to drive them away completely and give up the things you cherish most, word is you'll not only destroy your own life, but quite a few others in the process!"

"You're kidding."

"I don't think you were supposed to tell her all of that," Gene said.

"Well, they didn't say I couldn't. Valerie, it's really important you don't give in to the sciatica. It's really important that you believe in yourself."

She had fought both pain and drowsiness, listening to Fred's frightening prediction. But now the muscle relaxer kicked in fully, soothing her injured nerve. Val sighed, pulled the covers around herself, and shut her eyes.

"But I'm not a professional dancer," she murmured.

"Nobody said you have to be," she heard him answer. Then she drifted into welcomed sleep.

* * * *

She awoke in the late morning, the pain alternating between dull ache and sharp pulling jabs as she eased herself from bed. She fed Harpo, bending with exquisite care as she freshened his food and water, then she called the small ad firm she worked at, explaining her injury.

By one o'clock, the pain pills wore off. She called Michael and asked him to get her medicine for her. He came up, took her prescriptions, went out to fill them and brought them back.

She studied his kind, concerned face and wondered what he would think if she told him about Fred and Gene.

Michael lingered awkwardly. "Was Wayne here last night?"

She stared at him. "No. He doesn't know I injured myself yet. We came back from the hospital too late for me to call him, and I slept late this morning. Why?"

"I could have sworn I heard you talking to a man, once before you hurt yourself, and then after we came back, about two in the morning." He smiled sheepishly. "Must have been people next door."

"Must have been. There wasn't another living soul here last night."

"Well, call me if you need anything else."

"I will. Thanks, again, Mike. I owe you one. Big time."

"No, you don't. I'm just being a friend. Get some rest."

"I will." She let him out, took her medicine, then called Wayne. They'd been dating for almost three years now and had plenty in common. He taught literature at the university, but his tastes in music narrowed to traditional ballads and folk songs. He didn't dance. The few times Val tried to teach him panned out, his resistance as much in his mind as in his feet. Val danced alone.

Now she told Wayne about the sciatica. He listened, chagrined, then muttered, "This is why you need a better job. One with medical benefits."

"I'm trying, Wayne. It's only been a week since I interviewed at that law firm."

They talked for a while, until her pain pill kicked in. She told Wayne she needed to lie down, but as she hung up, her TV turned itself on.

She shuffled into the living room in time to see a movie starting: *Singin' in the Rain,* starring Gene Kelly, Debbie Reynolds and Donald O'Connor. Gene and his co-stars, replete with raincoats and umbrellas, grinned up at her from the screen.

She switched off the television and waited. No tap-dancing ghosts appeared. Satisfied, she limped back to bed and switched on her heating pad.

* * * *

The next morning, as her alarm clock buzzed shrilly, and she slowly swung her legs out of bed, her pain and stiffness gave her grave doubts about going to work. *I can't do this,* she thought.

"Yes, you can." Fred sauntered into her bedroom, hands in pockets. She would have jumped, had her muscles been willing. "The one thing those muscles need to heal *is* to move. Come on, get dressed. I'll accompany you to work, to help you keep your spirits up." She raised her eyebrows at his pun. He rubbed his chin.

Val grinned. "May I have a cup of coffee first?"

"You may, provided you don't go back to sleep, hide under the covers and refuse to face the light of day."

Val hobbled to the kitchen, to heat up the kettle.

Fred came in behind her and amazed her further by pulling back a chair and sitting down on it. "You disappointed Gene when you turned off his movie yesterday."

* * * *

Val panted as she limped with tiny, mincing steps to the bus stop. "Can anybody else out here see you?"

"Nope," Fred told her. "Nobody but you. So I suggest you stop talking to me aloud."

Val thought, *How am I supposed to talk to you?*

"Just like that," Fred answered her.

I'm crazy, she thought. The rest of the way he did all the talking, punctuated with frequent encouragement to keep her going, while she did the walking, punctuated by frequent rest stops to unstiffen her leg muscle and catch her hyperventilating breath.

Somehow she got through the workday, a walk to the bank to cash her meager paycheck, and back home. She ate a light supper, stripped down to step into a wonderfully hot shower, dried off, and slipped on her nightgown. She downed her medicine, then, nearly hugging the bed, fell fast asleep.

The next day, the kitchen radio awoke her. Val glanced at the clock: she had overslept by three hours. The radio channels kept changing themselves. *Here we go again,* she thought.

Gene, bent over the radio, looked up as she entered the kitchen. "Good morning. I'm searching for a relaxing station."

"Why didn't Harpo wake me?" she asked. "Harpo always wakes me if I oversleep."

"We told him not to disturb you," Fred said, walking in.

"And good morning to you, too," Val said.

"You're not going to work today. You were in a bit too much pain yesterday. We're letting you rest."

"And today's special," Gene added as the phone rang.

Val answered it gingerly. "Hello?"

"Valerie Robbins?"

"This is Valerie."

"This is Sheila Sims, from Personnel at Dunbar and Williams. You interviewed with us last week?"

"Oh, hello!"

"We're calling to offer you the job, Valerie, if you're still interested."

"You are?! I mean, yes! Yes, of course, I want the job."

"Mr. Williams will be just as pleased. You were his first choice among the candidates. How soon can you start?"

"Um, I'd like to give my current job two weeks' notice."

"That's fine. We'll see you in two weeks on Monday, October 30th. Report to me first. We'll need to fill out the usual forms, and then I'll take you over to Mr. Williams."

"I'll be there. And thanks again."

"You're welcome. See you then, Valerie."

They hung up, and Val beamed at Gene and Fred. "I've got the job!"

"Good benefits, too," Fred grinned.

"Now call Dr. John," Gene told her. "Uh, uh, uh! Stop worrying about money. He's good-hearted. He'll work it out with you. You need to heal up. You can't be limping around too long on your new job."

Val didn't ask how he knew her chiropractor's name. It seemed a moot point, coming from a ghost.

* * * *

After three weeks of ultrasound heat, electrical stimulation and adjustments (at one-third Dr. John's usual cost), Val still limped, but painlessly, with only slight discomfort. She joked about it with Sheila Sims, Mr. Williams and her new co-workers, toughing it out and working hard, quickly gaining their admiration.

Two months later, she stopped limping. Wayne came over on Saturday night as usual. "I suppose we should celebrate when you're feeling up to it," he said, impressed by her fortitude. "What would you like to do?"

Val's swung her legs over his lap as they sat on her couch. She took a deep breath. "Could we, um, go dancing?"

Wayne inched backwards into the couch cushion. "I wouldn't know where to go for that. I'm also not very good at it."

"You don't have to be. We could just go for an hour or so. I probably wouldn't be up to more than two or three slow dances, anyway."

He hesitated. "Well, if that's what you really want."

"Wayne, dancing is good for you. It's also romantic."

He sighed heavily. "Okay. We'll go next Saturday night. You choose where. Just promise me you won't overdo it, and I'll try not to trip over my two left feet."

* * * *

On Sunday morning she found Gene and Fred waiting patiently for her in her kitchen. She hadn't seen them for nearly three months. Fred lounged, smiling, against the wall. Gene relaxed in a chair, looking satisfied. "We came to applaud your stamina and swift recovery."

"I guess we could stop haunting you now," Fred added.

"Oh, I don't know. I kind of missed you," she admitted. "Besides, I still don't know why you, um, took such special interest in me." She paused shyly. "Am I supposed to become some great dancer…something along that line?"

Gene and Fred exchanged quick glances.

"Should we let her know?" Gene asked.

"Nah, better wait until the timing's right."

Val laughed, delighted by their repartee. "Wayne and I are going dancing next weekend."

"We know," said Fred.

"We'll be watching over," Gene said. "No doldrums."

"No doldrums," Val agreed.

* * * *

Val and Wayne arrived early at the club, Time After Time, before it became too crowded. He sat stiffly and ordered a ginger ale. Val had a sloe gin fizz. They sipped their drinks as the D.J. played some lively hits from the seventies and eighties. Despite her stiff leg, the music swirled in her head, her body responding to the rhythm. She wanted to dance, even if it cost her some soreness and an extra dose of heat rub in the morning. Finally a slow song, *Reunited,* came on. "Can we dance to this one?" she asked.

Wayne rose, his expression a mix of reluctance and bravery.

They moved around the floor slowly, Val guiding him in time to the beat. When he finally got the hang of it, the song ended. Wayne smiled wryly as they went back to their table.

Val sighed. She gazed longingly at other couples on the dance floor, then saw Gene and Fred heading towards her, weaving with quick rhythmic steps around the other dancers.

They raised their fingers to their lips, gesturing her to silence, then walked quietly to her table. Wayne sat there uncomfortably, a man out of his element, a penguin who'd been asked to try to fly.

A Gloria Estaban song, *You Made a Fool Out of Me,* a favorite of Val's, began to play. "I love this song. Can we dance to it?"

Gene headed toward them as they moved onto the dance floor. He came up behind Wayne, said, "May I?" reached out to him, and then suddenly disappeared.

"I seem to be getting the hang of this," Wayne grinned. He moved less woodenly to the music, his steps becoming more assured as he gently pivoted her around. They danced to the song without a single misstep.

Back at their table, Wayne relaxed, ordering another round of drinks. A vapor exuded from his back, reforming behind him. Gene dusted himself off and winked at her.

She wondered where Fred was, almost opening her mouth to ask, but Gene drew his finger swiftly up to his mouth. He pointed to the D.J.'s corner.

Fred leaned over the D.J.'s booth, talking to the man, who straightened up and began searching his CDs. He found the one he wanted and set it aside.

Fred headed back to her table. "Mind if we share the next dance with the lady?"

Wayne, unaware of Fred's presence, asked her, "What are you staring at?"

"I'm admiring the club decor."

"Ladies and Gentlemen," the D.J. announced, "we're going back to a time when dancing was supreme. See if you can start your bodies swaying to Frank Sinatra and *Come Dance with Me.*"

That number certainly wasn't a slow song; even Fred had faded at its mention. "I guess we can sit this one out."

"I don't see what for. The title is certainly appropriate. Shall we?" Wayne rose gallantly, took her hand and practically swept her onto the dance floor. He spun her around to the glamorous sound of the Big Band Era. Val glided along with him. She felt no pain, neither an ache nor a twinge, only the magic of the music.

The classic song ended. Val and Wayne hugged each other. She wondered at the sudden clapping until one woman complimented them and others echoed her praise.

Wayne laughed, both embarrassed and pleased. "I didn't know I had it in me," he told them, then led Val back to the table.

Val lifted her drink mid-high, silently toasting Fred and Gene, standing nearby on the dance floor. She took a sip and set her glass down.

Is the timing right? she mentally asked Fred.

"Oh, I think it might be. What do you think, Gene?"

"Mmn, I think these two will definitely be dancing together in the future."

Then, why? Val thought. Wayne's attention was centered on the other dancing couples, studying their steps.

Gene answered first. "Because you and Wayne will get married, and you'll have a child who'll inherit and be nurtured by your love of dancing, Val. That child will one day be a dancer as loved by its generation as Fred and I were by ours."

A thrill of awe and wonder swept over her.

Fred leaned over and put his arm gently around her shoulder. "Of course, that's not surprising, considering how this kid's future mother has already impressed us."

Thank you, she told them.

Gene, on Val's other side, bent down. He and Fred planted a kiss on each side of her cheek.

"Remember," Gene said, "always believe in yourself."

"By the way," Fred glanced at Wayne, "I'm glad he's a fast learner."

The two of them rose, walking arm in arm through the table and onto the dance floor. They faded off.

"Actually," Wayne said, "I'm beginning to enjoy this dancing business. It apparently isn't that hard after all."

Valerie wondered how he'd do the next time they took to the dance floor. "You pick the next one."

He chose *Born Again,* a slow song about the renewal of love and, Val thought, a second chance at life. Wayne relaxed into the lilting melody, feeling it, letting his feet follow its lead. Val had no difficulty matching his steps, as Wayne lowered his cheek, resting it against hers. "I wonder," he murmured. "If we got married and had a son, what would we name him?"

Val blinked. "Are you asking me to marry you?"

"I guess I am." He wore an endearingly lopsided grin.

"Then I accept."

His arms tightened around her. "So what will we name him?"

"Frederick?" Val offered, snuggling into his embrace, as romantic as any on a movie screen. "Then again, we might have a daughter first."

"A daughter?" Wayne smiled. "Well, my grandmother Jean was a great dancer."

"Oh. Was she a professional?"

"No, she just loved to dance. She and Grandfather Richard always drew a crowd when they hit the dance floor. I remember them trying to teach me to tap dance. I guess I just didn't inherit their talent."

"I wouldn't say that. You didn't do too badly on that last dance."

Wayne blushed. "I guess I do have a little rhythm in me. I'd be willing to learn, if it means that much to you."

Val tilted her head upward, locking gazes. "It means that much to me."

"Then I guess we'll have to do this more often, practice up for our wedding dance. Grandmother Jean used to have this saying, whenever someone said that they *had* to do something. She'd say: 'When the ears hear the music, the feet gotta dance.' And it always reminded me of that fairy tale about the Pied Piper. But now it reminds me of you. You've 'gotta dance.' It's part of your happiness, and I'll never take it from you."

As the song ended, and they reseated themselves, a twinge of pain pinched her lower back. Val stiffened.

"What's wrong, Val?"

"Just got a jab."

"Okay." He looked at his watch. "I think it's time to head home and let you get some sleep. Tell those feet of yours that we'll be dancing again in the future."

That gained him a kiss. They walked slowly to his car and drove to her apartment. Wayne helped her upstairs and gave her back the kiss, insisting that Val get a good night's rest. Val reluctantly let him go, and stood by the front window, looking out as Wayne drove away, watching his car lights fade.

She turned away from the window and thought she saw Fred and Gene sitting on the couch, smiling at her. But it was just a trick of her peripheral vision and late night weariness.

She lay down on the couch, thinking of how good it would be when she and Wayne were married, when *going home* meant to *their home*. Together. She dozed off into a dream. In it, she and Wayne were out walking on a sun-lit spring day with their four kids of varying ages: two boys and two girls.

The sight of all those kids jolted Val awake. She sat up abruptly on the couch, remembering what Gene and Fred had told her: she and Wayne would have a *kid* who'd grow up to be a dancer. Not four kids. Just one. So if they had more than one, how would she know *which* one? She *wouldn't* know, at least not until he—or she—grew up and became famous.

Oh, dear, Val thought, all those dance slippers and tap shoes.

She mentally cast her puzzlement toward the Great Beyond, but if Fred and Gene heard her, all she got back was a gentle trickle of emotion, mixing patience and anticipation with amusement.

THE GREATER THIRST

The night will end soon. So few hours to write down my story. The Philadelphia police will record it, no doubt, as a grisly hoax tied in with a bizarre and unsolved murder. They will not see it as a tribute to Sarah, a paean extolling her final triumph over me, and as final proof of my love for her.

They don't believe in vampires.

Nor did Sarah, until we met here in Philadelphia, in the halcyon year of 1965. Sarah was an art student attending the Pennsylvania Academy of Fine Arts. I had recently moved to the city of brotherly love, keeping my true name, Darien Longwood, but setting up a revised identity, purchasing a new set of legal records. I had financed the subterfuge, thickly greasing the palms of its perpetrators by privately selling a handful of my possessions which had long since become antiques. I then leased a beautiful, historic row house at 19th and Delancey Streets near Rittenhouse Square, a few blocks from where Sarah Cantrell rented a small apartment on 21st Street. In the evenings, she frequented a pleasant coffeehouse, The Gilded Cage, which was where I first saw her.

She didn't strike me as beautiful, but rather as an alluring woman. She caught my interest quickly, as sudden lightning in a calm night sky would.

She sat, alone and apparently contented, at a corner table, sipping tea, and watching an overweight, middle-aged man hunched over his chair, picking and strumming a competent version of Debussy's *Clair de Lune* on his guitar.

I sat at a corner table diagonally across from her. She appeared to be of average height, perhaps five feet six, her figure trim, but not slender. She wore a sleeveless, dark blue shift that hung lazily on her. The hem flowed around her crossed legs, ending just above her knees. Her feet were shod in black cloth, flat-heeled shoes. Her skin was coffee au lait-colored, a dark gold which I surmised was natural. Although unseasonably warm, it was still spring, few people attaining full tans (I smiled as I thought this). This woman's flesh was richly and evenly hued. Her hair was a sable brown, long, and sleek with waves. Her eyes, also brown, were lighter, nearly chestnut. She had a long nose, its base small, and high cheekbones.

I entered her mind. I found this ability, to read human thoughts, to be useful, but rarely pleasurable. Human minds can be grotesque or sublime, corrupted or pure, commonplace or unique, motives and intentions, hopes and disappointments spread out before us, as in a feast. We vampires cling to life, covet every morsel we can siphon in our mocking sojourn. If you fail to amuse us, you are in danger. Common wine. You unwittingly compound the boring trap we fell into when we became immortal. If you lengthen the evening interminably, a reminder of endless nights to come, it could well be your last.

If you challenge us, you may, unlike us, see the dawn. You have fed us in ways other than the blood and are therefore valuable *alive.* If you are rare and can touch our darkness, bringing sunlight at midnight…that, my friend, presents a quagmire. A thirst deeper than blood will expose our weak spot, where you can pierce us. Such human gems are never relegated to slavery, never chattel to our will. Their indomitable affection for their mortal path thwarts our control.

We seek them out for our new generation. They often resist us, while equally attracted to us. They deal with us gingerly, fluttering like moths near hot night lamps, keeping their distance to avoid burnt wings. We employ every ruse, every deceit, every gamble, to capture them, bringing their bright souls into our burning darkness for eternity.

Sarah's mind swirled with music, colors, shapes, a vibrancy exceedingly rare in most people, raising that which she sensed to the heightened state we call *art.*

Sarah Cantrell was not merely listening to the guitarist's rendition of *Claire de Lune.* She was merging with the notes, incorporating them into her mind, touching them, tasting them, encircling them as a musical whole. She was *becoming Claire de Lune,* and becoming Debussy, experiencing his composition's birth and completion, as if she were the composer. She had heard its haunting melody many times before. Yet each rendition mesmerized her.

I rose, crossed the room, and sat down at her table across from her.

"You appear to be an enthusiast of classical music," I said. "So am I. May I join you?"

She stared at me briefly before replying. "Yes, I am. Debussy, Rachmaninoff, and Tchaikovsky are my favorites. And I suppose there's no harm in your sitting there."

I laughed. "But I may be a very dangerous fellow, for all you know."

"Not in a well-lit place."

I smiled. "Are you a musician?"

"No. An artist." When I waited, quietly attentive, she continued. "I'm a student at the Pennsylvania Academy of the Fine Arts. I graduate in June."

"Really? What do you paint?"

"Oh, people, scenes from nature. I'm not big on still life. I tend towards realism and emotionalism, although I can appreciate the modern forms, the abstract and the cubist. I suppose I'm a bit old-fashioned in my style and subject matter."

"And your mentors? Who has influenced your artwork?"

She laughed. "You're full of questions. Well, I originally studied the impressionists. I still love the works of Toulouse-Lautrec, and Van Gogh makes me shiver. He's so *intense!* Do you know that his early works and his final works are filled with equal passion? There was this retrospective of his I was lucky enough to attend in Paris. It was my first trip to Europe and the Louvre had put together a showing of his paintings. Two of his canvases stood out intensely. I'll never forget them."

She fell silent, caught up in the memory.

"Which ones?" I asked her.

"One was *The Potato Eaters,* done when he was working as a minister among the miners. This impoverished family was seated around a table in a very dark room, lit centrally by candlelight, as they talked and laughed, and ate, of course, potatoes. But their faces, the light suffusing them in the darkness, made them appear almost holy, touched by God. The final painting was Vincent's last before he shot himself, of blackbirds in a darkening sky. The blackbirds seemed to come at you, a storm of wings, cawing finality, the end of all things. Death."

She had been gazing distantly off as she spoke. I had gone into her mind, viewing these works as she pictured them, seeing them touched by her fervor. Now she shook off the memory, returning to the present. "Lord, I'm sorry. I must sound morbid."

"No, not at all. I have seen these paintings. They are as superb as your descriptions imply."

She beamed. "Then you know what I'm talking about."

"Yes."

She regarded me quietly. "I'm Sarah Cantrell."

"I'm pleased to meet you, Miss Cantrell. My name is Darien Longwood."

"Sarah, please. There's no need for such formality in this day and age."

I nodded. "Sarah, then."

"Pleased to meet you as well, Darien," she said. "And what do you do? What's your claim to fame?"

"I'm a vampire," I admitted in an extremely low voice, leaning close to her, "but a very cultured one."

Not a muscle of her body moved. Her eyes flickered to mine, lowered and then rose to meet my gaze again. She smiled, slowly and uncertainly.

"You're a darned good actor. I almost believe you," she said, her smile stretching to a smirk.

After much persuasion, mainly my assurance that I was not deranged, she allowed me to walk her home.

I probed her, rather egotistically, to see how she pictured me. She took me for a suave, rather controlled man of a few years older than herself, in my mid to late twenties. She believed me possessed of a droll, comedic streak and expected further antics from me, evidencing my wry, humorous nature. I did intend to stage a diversion, but one which would force her to confront my vampiric nature.

We continued up 19th Street, Sarah turning her head every now and then to gaze at me in a natural and relaxed manner. I knew she was curious about my "real" background, and wondering why I chose to act mysterious. I also caught glimpses of myself within her thoughts, and was pleased with the picture her mind rendered of me, a vampire's mirror.

She liked my six-foot frame, the rich onyx shading and moderate cut of my hair, and the way one lock dangled over my forehead. She thought my square facial shape, strong nose and full mouth enticingly masculine, and found my dark eyes a complement to my fair complexion. She approved of my taste in clothes, currently black trousers, matching leather loafers, a white cotton shirt, and a brown suede tailored jacket. She thought it a happy coincidence that she preferred broad-chested men who were sturdy but trim. She wondered if I harbored comparable attractions between my legs, and decided that I must.

The lit display of an expensive dress shop arrested her attention as we approached it. The mannequin within it wore a red silk evening dress generously studded with rhinestones. Its skirt was fashionably short.

Sarah stared at the dress longingly.

"Do you like it?" I asked her.

She frowned. "I couldn't afford it on a student's income. My budget's strained to the hilt as it is."

"I'll get it for you."

"Will you? You ought to get to know a woman better, before you start buying clothes for her. I might be one of the wily females who use men for their money."

"I didn't say I was going to buy it."

"What are you going to do? Steal it?"

I paused, considering how she might react. "I prefer the term 'requisition' to that of 'theft.' I need to ask something of you. You are to stand here and not move. No matter what you see, remain here, and wait for me. I promise you no harm shall come to you, nor any shame. When my theatrics are complete—for I can see you believe I am being theatrical—you shall have your dress. Do I have your agreement?"

She hesitated, her eyes troubled, then nodded.

"Good," I said. "Now remember: don't move from this spot, no matter what you see."

I began my shape-shifting then, in front of her, my body fading slowly, its atoms rearranging under my direction, until I became transparent, and then a ghostly outline, and finally, conscious mist.

I seeped my gaseous form through the space beneath the locked doorway of the dress shop, entered its darkened interior, and returned myself to human form behind the door. Carefully switching off the alarm system, I climbed up into the bay of the display window and removed the red silk dress. Flinging it over my arm, I turned to Sarah, who watched with dumbfounded eyes, her mouth a perfect O, on the opposite side of the plate glass. I waved.

Behind the sales counter, I found garish plastic bags imprinted with the store's name and its flowery logo. I carefully noted the price of the dress—$85.00—and rang it up on the cash register. And bagging the dress for Sarah, I let myself out, first resetting the alarm and pristinely locking the door behind me.

I held out the package containing her prize. She backed a step away from me, her eyes searching up and down my body, then moved forward, reaching for the bag.

We walked mutely down 19th Street, then cut left onto Walnut.

"How did you do that?" she finally asked.

"I've told you. I'm a vampire."

She was silent at first, then, "Or perhaps a master illusionist setting up an innocent dupe."

I walked slightly ahead of her and stopped under the sharp glow of a streetlamp. She caught up and stood under its light.

Taking her hand, I brought it to my mouth.

She flinched.

"I will not harm you. I won't do anything to you without your acquiescence."

She relaxed.

I parted my lips and brushed her fingertip over one elongated frontal incisor, pausing on its needle point, then the other. I lowered her hand. "Perhaps a master illusionist with two false teeth."

"Nothing against my will?"

"Nothing without your expressed consent."

She continued walking.

I fell in beside her. "I find you enticing…and puzzling. You're not really afraid of me. In fact, you're intrigued and willing to risk the adventure of my acquaintance."

She stopped again and stared at me. "How did you—," she began, then halted, making a decision. "A painting I'm working on at my apartment might possibly express why I'm not afraid of you. Startled, perhaps, but not afraid."

We were silent the rest of the way. Even her mind remained silent, except for images of the painting she wished to show me, which I could only glean in segments: a languid hand, the vision of a rose, a woman's face in flickering shadows.

We approached a small greystone building, its outer entrance containing a walled, shadowed alcove, which I noted for future use when stalking. Sarah fumbled in her pocket and withdrew her keys. We entered a drab hallway and climbed to the second floor. Another lock turned, and we were in her apartment.

She switched on the living room light. In one corner was a niche containing her easel with her canvas on it, and a kitchen cart. The cart's top shelf was filled with brushes, tubes of paint, willow reed charcoal, and bottles of linseed oil and turpentine. Its bottom shelf held stretched canvases stacked according to size, sketch pads, and two spray cans of fixative and varnish.

Against the wall, across from the doorway, a small bed was covered with a floral comforter and heaped with pillows. To the right of the entrance, a chest of drawers stood, followed by a captain's chair which faced the room's one window. Below the window a small television sat on a long bookcase, its shelves packed to overflowing. Off to the left of the doorway were two small rooms, a bathroom and a kitchenette, and between them, a closet.

I walked over to her makeshift studio, to her work-in-progress. It was nearly finished, barring a well-sketched rose, its petals, stems and leaves unpainted.

"Now you can answer a question that puzzles *me,*" Sarah said. "Why does death court and claim people who haven't fully lived yet?"

The fragmented elements of her painting, seen flickering in her mind, coalesced before me. A woman approximating Sarah's age sprawled half-on, half-off a darkly-upholstered plush sofa. Her blind but staring blue eyes, the laxity of the rosebud mouth, the rigidity of her posture were unflinchingly portrayed. Whoever she was, she was beautiful. She lay on her stomach, head turned to the viewer, arm trailing the rug, the fingers of her hand spread, as if they reached for the rose.

"She was my friend Natalie," Sarah said. "She seemed to have this love for life that I often envied, a really positive can-do attitude. She drew people to her, both male and female. She never lacked for company, never seemed worried or troubled. Then one night she…up and took a mess of barbiturates. Then she called me. I don't know, maybe she changed her mind, didn't want to die. But she didn't say, 'Come over. I've just taken an overdose of drugs.' No cry for help. Just told me it was important, to get over there immediately. She sounded funny, and when I asked if she was okay, she just said she wasn't feeling well. When I got there, I knocked and I knocked, and finally I tried the door. It was unlocked. I went inside and I found her just like that, except there was no rose. The rose symbolizes life. I believe she was reaching for life when she called me, called for me."

She fell mute.

"I'm very sorry to hear about your friend," I said. "Did she leave a note or some other indication explaining her suicide?"

"No. No, nothing. Somehow I had to both accept her death and resurrect her. The rose is that symbol, because the bush it stems from blooms again in the spring."

I regarded her with cruel amusement. "Then you haven't accepted death. Those who die an ordinary death are lost forever."

"That's not true." She firmly locked eyes with me. "I believe in another world, another dimension, a continuation of the soul."

She told me of her father, who had died when Sarah was fifteen, and of her waking dream in which his soul had come to her and told her not to grieve.

"An illusion of your mind," I grimly refuted her. "I have died. There is nothing beyond for mortals. Even a rose bush dies if its roots are torn from the earth."

* * * *

Sarah believed in a fatuous god who controlled a universe both physical and spiritual. She was certain her friend Natalie had been resurrected, and that she, too, would be transported into a greater world upon her own death. I asked her then why her god had created vampires. She answered that I was damned, most probably for some spiritual infraction, and condemned to walk the earth until I found atonement.

The waging of our philosophical battle became a challenge to her, as I knew it would. I argued with her many a night, until her eyes drooped and I left her to her rest; as a mortal, she had to face the day.

Our strange alliance of vampire and mortal continued for two years. I both fascinated and repelled her. She couldn't face the empty darkness I insisted human death led to. She insisted I had brought that darkness upon myself, had robbed myself of something greater. I denied this, defying her at some intrinsic, primal level, and by her reaction, knew that I would win.

She had graduated from the Academy, taking a job as a layout artist for an advertising firm while continuing her fine art career on the side. Her superb canvases soon found favor and fortune among regional art galleries, and Sarah began painting full-time.

I waited patiently for the moment, the event that would bring Sarah into my world, my *coup de grace*. My patience was rewarded. Sarah's mother died in a senseless and sudden auto crash.

On the evening following her mother's funeral, I waited, uninvited, for Sarah at her apartment. My unexpected presence only momentarily startled her.

"Have you come to gloat?" she asked. The acid in her tone disturbed me.

"No, I've come to comfort you."

"You?"

"Do you think I like death any more than you do? I've held it back for over two centuries!"

She didn't answer, kicking off her black pumps, and undoing her long brown hair from the tightened prim upsweep she had styled it in. I rose and went over to her, helping her remove the pins, smoothing and untangling the strands.

"Sarah," I said, "do you doubt that I fear the day death will steal you from me, steal your talent and your courage, steal the wonderment and vibrancy you bring into my endless life? If I had my way, you would never die, my sweet lady, you would live forever."

"I will. But not in the world you inhabit."

"So you say. But I know you won't survive. Not unless you accept and return the vampiric kiss."

She faced me, her soft eyes blazing with released anger. "And will you instruct me on my first kill in this vampiric afterlife of yours? And on how to cover up the death by making it look like a crime of violence? Is that what I'm worth to you?"

"I would protect you. Eternally."

"You once said you would never thwart my will. I want you to go and never return."

"And leave you to face death alone?"

"The loneliness won't last long."

"But the darkness will last forever, Sarah."

"You're the one who lives in darkness."

"But I live."

She began to cry, turning her tear-streaked face away from me. I probed her thoughts. She had no brothers nor sisters, and only distant relatives.

"Let me take care of you, Sarah. I'll be your family, your home, your hearth."

"Why are you doing this to me? Why are you being so cruel?"

"Because I love you," I answered her softly. "And because you love me."

"Love," she muttered, wiping her eyes with the back of her hand. "What makes you think I love you?"

"It's been nearly two years, Sarah. Why have you refused every other man's advances?"

"How do you know what I've done with other men? You're not here every night."

"I know. Or do you deny what I've said is true?"

The tension between us quickened, and I, who am succored by blood, felt her essence, her blood, flow toward me. "You once wondered if I could sexually satisfy you, if I would *measure up*. I cannot. I share life in my own manner. Will you share it with me, save yourself from the darkness to come, and bring your light to the darkness of my nights?"

I felt her acquiesce before she slowly lifted her gaze to my face. From her eyes, a fresh flow of tears descended, then she was suddenly in my arms.

I stroked her through the night, and when I sensed her readiness, I lowered my lips to her neck, suckling and kissing her, and then drew the sweetness of her life into my veins until she hung on mortality's periphery. Then pierced my own neck for her to drink back the nectar of our mingled blood.

* * * *

In the days that followed, I made good on my promise, shielding her and easing Sarah carefully into her vampiric life. I moved her belongings into my Delancey Street home, and when she thirsted, I carefully chose a victim and rendered the mortal unconscious out of Sarah's sight. Then, she would drink until sated, and wander off while I disposed of the kill.

Through vampiric friends and human consorts, we spread a plausible story, with a doctor's diagnosis backing it up, of Sarah's developing a sensitivity to sunlight. She continued to paint and exhibit her work, but receptions were only held in the fall and winter months, and the artist always arrived fashionably late.

We continued to debate theology, as a pleasant game of intellectual thrusting and sparring. I should have realized the change when it came over her, for Sarah began to make sarcastic, snide remarks on beliefs she once held sacred while mortal. When I teased her chidingly about it, she gaily explained she was playing God's Advocate for the sport of it.

Sarah's paintings also changed. Instead of celebrating life, they depicted its emptiness. One painting particularly disturbed me, of homeless street children scrounging in a trash bin. Food did not seem their aim. One small girl stood off from the rest, holding a prize she had requisitioned. She held the red silk dress, torn and stained.

"Where *is* the red silk dress?" I asked.

Sarah shrugged her shoulders, busily varnishing the canvas. "You'll recall I wore it to my last opening. Some eager young admirer spilled wine on it. I did throw it out."

When I further questioned the altered mood and subjects of her latest paintings, she shrugged that off, too, but not without a hint of bristling.

"You brought me to darkness. Did you think that wouldn't affect my work? Or did you think I'd remain Little Mary Sunshine, forever lighting your eternal nights?"

"Do you still love me? Or has that, too, changed?"

She hesitated, and I saw the vampire's ennui cross her face. "No," she said, "I still love you."

To this very moment, the ambivalence of her answer still haunts me. She had changed, and I was responsible. Her sacrifice had never been complete.

Love often isn't enough.

* * * *

Sarah had been hunting with me, but soon took to stalking without me. She decided the civilized world was far too logical to believe in vampires, just as she had not, before our meeting, and that law enforcement officers would miss the closed punctures in her victims' throats, or mistake them for skin eruptions. She was careful not to deplete her victims' blood to the point of high suspicion.

In the master bedroom of the town house, she slept in an antique four-poster, completely surrounded by a thick black velvet bed curtain. The shutters on the room's two windows were tightly locked from the inside and inner curtains covered them, allowing no daylight in. Snug in her black velvet tomb, she insisted she was safe. I felt no such assurance, and slept in my coffin in the basement, fastening it from within.

She began to work on a painting she said would please me, because it had the vibrancy, the unadulterated honesty she knew I craved and relished in her art. She insisted I not see it while it progressed, at first making me suspicious, for we had never hid anything from each other before. But she allayed my worries by treating the mystery as if it augured a wonderful surprise.

I could no longer read her thoughts, for she had learned the trick of vampirically blocking them, although she had rarely employed it with me until now. I did not block my own from her. Perhaps that was why she became arduously attentive to my other needs and desires, taking delight in the smallest pleasures, communicating her excited innocence, mesmerizing me with the brightness of her view.

They were the happiest weeks of my immortal life. I began to look forward to the unveiling of the painting, believing it presaged a new era of contentment between us.

And so I rose in good spirits early that Sunday evening in November and searched the house for her. I finally climbed to the renovated attic where she'd set up her studio, insisting jocularly that she needed strong northern light. To humor her, I hired carpenters to install two large, opposing bay windows, one overlooking Delancey Street, the other, our courtyard garden, filled with night blooms.

The door to the attic was left slightly ajar, but no sound came from within.

"Sarah?"

No response.

I quietly opened the door to her studio.

The easel sat in the middle of the spacious room, its back to me. The sheet with which Sarah had draped the newest painting to conceal it from me lay in a heap on the floor behind the easel.

The painting, exposed and unguarded, rested on it.

I hesitated. Would she be angry if I viewed the work before she wished me to? Or had she planned this, the sheet not falling by accident?

I decided to risk her displeasure, stepping around the easel to view her work.

The scene before the easel halted me mid-step. A horrid pile of clothing, bones and dust lay on the polished, hardwood floor.

The skull laughed at me, a short distance from the jumbled remains of the woman I had thought would stay beside me forever.

Sarah, obtaining her long-coveted, steathily planned release, had in doing so abandoned me. Fury coursed through me, a twisting spiral. Grief also swelled, commingling like lightning within a tornado's funnel, crashing against the unaged flesh of my body, trapped within me, unreleased.

I reached down and picked up the blue shift she had worn the day we met. A belated reminder to me that I had not won. Had never won.

Even the black cloth shoes she had worn lay at odd angles near fragmented bits of fibula and tibia.

Remnants of Sarah's hipbone and vertebrae broke free of the blue cloth as I brought it to my lips, the brittle bone shattering to pieces at my feet. I clutched the dress to me, in pain, but couldn't cry.

The pain of loss, unwilling, tormented loss, seared literally through my chest. I found myself heaving for renewed breath. With fierce effort, I regained control, and mentally envisioned Sarah's final, desperate act, an act designed both to return her to the light, and to force me, whom she truly loved, to honestly face myself.

I gazed at the portrait, its oils still wet upon the canvas, and remembered Sarah's leave-taking the night before, as she planted a lingering kiss upon my lips and cast a hungering, aching glance my way, pleading with a small smile for time alone to finish her masterpiece.

"Will I see it soon?" I had asked.

"Yes. Very soon," she had replied.

She had gone into the studio then, to complete her work. Had she sat by the bay windows, gazing up at the night sky, seeing stars amid the blackness? Had she watched the sun come up, an ending triumph? I know she had stood before the portrait, at the last—studying my face, perhaps hoping the message she had left, embedded in my portrait, would be understood— as daylight streamed into the studio, claiming her.

I stared at my likeness upon the canvas. Her brushwork and careful use of color assured me that she found me handsome and sensitive. But that elusive gift that heightens talent into genius had saturated the canvas with a hitherto unspeakable shade of truth.

She had painted me caught in a web of stagnation, of crippling, restricting ennui, the spidery web extending from my shoulders, head, and neck. The eyes that looked out at mine cried for release, saw the future as eternal emptiness, eternal loneliness, seeking out others like Sarah, to trap in my eternal hell.

I know now. I can only rob them of that which I crave if I succeed.

Yet the somber hues juxaposed and blended with highlights of luminous gold-yellow and pale azure told me of her belief in me, of my ability to resurrect myself, not merely through the blood of my victims, but through the more terrifying, fiercer sacrifice of faith.

I held the cup before me, and sought to fill it to the brim, but that which was within it turned sour at my touch.

I stare at myself and know it is Sarah and her freedom I crave.

This epitaph is done.

I can feel the first faint rays of dawn approaching.

THE PRICK RETURNS

Tony always called him The Prick. After Bryan died, we'd sit around stoned, and Tony would joke that if anyone came back from the dead, it would be Bryan with his prodigious appetite for drugs, booze, and broads.

Bryan was the larger-than-life lead singer in our band. I always thought if Bryan hadn't died we might have made it. The big time. Bryan was the musical genius of our group, although he preferred singing to playing. When he was gone, the gigs slowly went the way of the grave, too. No replacement ever measured up.

But I couldn't voice that opinion to Tony. Tony's jealousy of anyone more talented than him made him unduly critical of others. A lot of people had more talent than Tony.

So we're sitting in our rented home in a South Philadelphia housing project, eating breakfast about three weeks after Bryan kicked the proverbial bucket, crashing his Volkswagen Beetle into a truck while driving high. It's 1969 and autumn is providing some color to our look-a-like neighborhood, but the Halloween decorations don't help. We're each glum, grieving in our weird ways; Tony because he'll never be more than a mediocre drummer and Bryan's performance at least masked that fact; Greg because Bryan encouraged his development as a lead guitarist, and without him, Greg's insecurity is back; Mike, a good bass player, because he was Bryan's closest friend, even if he was gay and loved Bryan, who was completely straight. And me because Bryan was my friend and protected me from Tony's abusive behavior.

I'm glad Greg and Mike spend most of their time at our place. They also help keep Tony's temper under control. Greg's asleep on the couch. Mike's eating breakfast with Tony and me. Our four-year-old daughter is still upstairs in her room.

I finish my toast and coffee, rinse my dishes in the sink and start toward the living room. Tony looks up from his cereal bowl. "Where ya goin', Julie?"

I half-turn. "To the john. All right with you?"

He nods, dismissing me. I climb the stairs, go in the bathroom and answer nature's call, then start to comb my long auburn hair into something neater than a sleep-mussed tangle. I lower my eyes from the mirror as I pull my hair back and rubber-band it into a low ponytail. When I raise my eyes again to the mirror, Bryan smiles back at me in its reflection, as if he's right beside me. I whirl around. No one's there. I turn back to the mirror. Only my own shocked reflection stares back at me.

"Bryan," I whisper. Silence answers, but then I feel the slightest caress on my cheek and a gentle tug on my ponytail. And think, *damn!*

And a thought comes into my head that I swear isn't my own: *It's not that bad being dead, Julie.*

The reason I think I'm seeing things, imagining Bryan there, is that I'm congenitally blind, legally blind, having no lenses. They were cut when I was a little kid during cataract surgery. I can't see straight on. I can only see peripherally from the corner of my eyes. But it compensates, and I can even read, slowly, my head tilted, from that corner. I went through the whole rigmarole of training with the local school for the blind, learning how to cope, how to compensate, how to survive and get around. Can't drive but I can navigate streets and public transportation.

Tony and I have a son, seven years old, also congenitally blind, and Tony, Jr. lives with my father and my Mom at my father's insistence. Better life and all that jazz, except that it's true, even if they also live in this housing project, a few blocks away. Tony's not the best parent, and my father hates my husband.

Our daughter, Carrie, is fully-sighted. I protect her from Tony's temper. He knows there are things I'll put up with, but I draw the line with Carrie. Tony's a half-assed husband and father, but he's got a nasty ace up his sleeve. If I complain about his behavior, he threatens to take Tony, Jr. away from my parents. If he did, my father would freak.

Carrie's the only one who seems together about Bryan's death. I told her the truth, softening it with the bit about his going to Heaven. She just looked at me somberly and nodded. I pass her small room. She's sitting on her bed, talking softly.

I lean against the doorway. "Honey."

She turns, somewhat startled, and puts a finger dramatically to her lips. "Ssh. Bryan's here. He came back from Heaven to see us."

I worry about her telling Tony and facing his sarcasm and anger. "That's good, but don't tell anyone else, okay? It'll be our secret."

"That's what Bryan said, not to tell anyone but you, Mommy."

And in my head, I hear Bryan again: *Yes, keep it secret.*

* * * *

Two weeks later, Tony starts taking his frustrations out on me again, beating me whenever Greg and Mike aren't around. He avoids my face, so it won't show. Carrie hides in her room when Daddy gets violent with

Mommy, an unspoken rule. I try to block Tony's punches, but don't shout. Silent suffering for Carrie's sake.

That's when I find out Bryan is still protecting me.

Tony's short but wiry and strong. He and Bryan both had long, blond hair and blue eyes, but Bryan was a few inches taller and somehow looked handsome and hot, while Tony comes off runty. Tony always wanted to score with girls at our gigs, but Bryan always won the prize groupies. That pissed Tony off. He'd push me around, whenever he lost an opportunity to cheat.

I was never unfaithful. Not out of love. Life wasn't great, but I preferred it to being dead. So far, the abuse was survivable.

Stupid things trigger Tony's temper. Like something I said or a look that someone gives him, or his jealous imagination, or his ego needing a rise and getting one by bullying me.

Tony gets me on the bed, striking my stomach and worse, and it hurts where he hits. I double up into a fetal position, expecting him to swing me back for another blow. But he screams and when I turn and look at him, he's off the bed, hopping around the bedroom, his left hand cupped over his left eye, shouting, "Son of a bitch, son of a bitch! Something's wrong with my eye! It feels like someone slugged it!" When he lowers his hand, his eye is swollen and discolored.

"Better get some ice on that," I mutter, "whatever caused it."

He storms out and heads down the stairs to the kitchen. And I feel a gentle caress on my cheek, and I *know*. I send Bryan a silent *thank you*.

* * * *

At this point, Bryan avoids any ghostly activity around Greg and Mike, but not around Tony, doing silly haunting things to irritate him, like shutting doors, making lights flicker, and moving things that were in another place a minute ago. So Tony starts saying we have a ghost, and we have to hold a séance to find out who it is. Mike says maybe the ghost is Bryan, but Tony says no, it isn't Bryan, that Bryan's chasing all the babe devils in Hell and wouldn't bother with the likes of us anymore. So he arranges a séance to identify the ghost.

I have to stifle my laughter as we all sit around the kitchen table: me, Greg, Mike, Tony, a dark-haired girl named Sue that Tony picked up at our last gig (his current lover, no secret there), and a neighbor we're friendly with named Ken. Ken fancies himself a wizard and is lately initiating Tony in the fine art of mystical bullshit. Although I believe in the paranormal, these guys act like it's a game with no rules. They tried contacting Bryan's spirit before, but Bryan wouldn't play.

They say when you lose one sense, you gain another. Maybe that's why

I can sort of see Bryan, out of the corner of my eye, as he smiles wickedly, leaning against the kitchen counter, watching this crazy séance. I clamp my lips shut to keep from smiling back at him and lower my gaze to the table, as Ken lights the candles in the evening gloom and clasps hands with Sue and me, and we clasp our hands with the others. He begins, solemn as a funeral director: "We ask that the spirit haunting this house make his presence known, that we may help it to find peace and go to the light."

Everyone is all seriousness as Ken tries to reach our ghost. "We beseech thee, spirit. Tell us what year you lived in!"

Ken tries again. "Give us a sign that you are receptive to us, oh, spirit."

I look at our real ghost. Bryan just stands there, arms folded, looking amused, apparently not interested in satisfying Ken and Tony's egos with the expected parlor trick.

"Spirit," Ken says, a bit impatiently, "we need a sign."

And Tony growls caustically, "Give us a sign, spirit!" Silence surrounds us. Then Tony suddenly mouths off, voice and temper rising: "You know, mother fucker, I've been putting up with your stupid tricks for weeks now, and you only pull them on me, and you fuckin' don't show up for no one else, just me. And I wanta know who the fuck you are and I wanta know it *now!*" Then he jumps up, breaking the circle, shrieking: "REVEAL YOURSELF, YOU PRICK!"

Then we all can't help exploding with laughter, laughter that goes on and on until you practically fall off your chair and can hardly breathe.

Only I can see Bryan, doubled up with his own laughter. Only I can see and hear him as he grins and suddenly straightens up, flinging his arms wildly outward, snapping his fingers, and smugly announcing: *"Well, snap my sheets! The Prick is* IN!"

Tony's explosion still has everyone else wracked with spasms of laughter. They don't know that Bryan's joke has started me laughing again, banging my fists on the table. The circle is broken and the séance over, and the ghost has a new name. The only name Tony ever calls him now: *The Prick.*

* * * *

Ken takes me over to his house to meet a girl, a musician who'd been friends with Bryan in high school. I can't picture Bryan being only *friends* with a woman, but apparently Melanie and he were, drifting apart after graduation. Bryan walked on the wild side; Melanie played it safe. A month before he died, they met up again. Bryan pursued her romantically. Melanie, despite her attraction to him, held him at arm's length.

She didn't know about our band; he never mentioned it, only saying he still worked some gigs as a musician, renewing other passions with her, going to a movie, the art museum, listening to Melanie's original songs, which she played for him at her Center City apartment, and her collection of jazz, folk and blues records.

She read about his sudden death in the City Paper, shocking her, and realized she had loved him.

The City Paper mentioned our band. When she met Ken in Rittenhouse Square, he told her he knew Bryan and our band. He brings her to meet us, and I can see Bryan standing behind her, a petite girl with a Kewpie Doll face and brown hair. He's pointing at her, and only I can see and hear him say: *She's the one!* I don't know what he means.

We're standing in Ken's kitchen as Ken's wife feeds their year-old son. Ken introduces her to us. I immediately like her, especially when she corners me and says, "Bryan told me about you, Julie, said you were a musician friend of his who, despite being blind, was a good keyboardist and rhythm guitarist. He also said you write songs. I do too. I'd love to hear some of yours."

"Maybe later," I tell her, cheered by the praise, "but I thought you didn't know about our band."

"I didn't. Bryan never mentioned anyone but you." She keeps staring at the long sleeves of my blouse, even though it's autumn and cool enough for them. They cover the bruises Tony left. And she whispers, "Ken told me Tony's beating you, Julie. You can't put up with that."

I'm glad Tony's in the living room. Melanie's just met me. She's taking liberties, but I allow it because there's this *déjà vu* connection with her. And it's not like she's going to *do anything* about Tony. Talk is cheap; it's a girlfriend thing, earnest advice and all that crap.

Then Tony suggests we all go back to our house and order a pizza for dinner. It's Saturday night and the mood is right, especially since we smoked some pot earlier and we've got the munchies. So Ken tells his wife that he'll be at our place, and we all head there.

I walk beside Melanie. She still seems out of place. I wonder if she ever smoked a reefer or did any other drugs, and all of a sudden Bryan is beside me and tells me no, she never did. I get the feeling she wouldn't like it, she seems too straight, no high limbs for her to climb out on. Then she leans close to me and says in a whisper, "I don't know if you believe in this stuff, but Bryan's been haunting me."

I whisper back, "Are you afraid?"

"Actually, no. He's the nicest ghost I've ever dealt with."

At which point, I think, ho-kay…what's going on here?

And Bryan adds his own whisper: *She's going to help you, Julie.*

* * * *

Sue is at the house because she's living there. Tony moved her in. She's in the living room with Greg, Mike and Carrie. Mike sits on the rug with Carrie, helping her crayon in her coloring book.

Tony grabs Sue and gives her a sloppy kiss, making her giggle as she watches my reaction. Sue has her own mean streak. She's too stupid to realize I'm beyond caring. Melanie's eyebrows raise and she scowls at him. I make introductions and lead her into the kitchen to show her my electric guitar in the corner.

Immediately, Tony's jealous. He doesn't like me commandeering new women who don't pay attention to him first. Melanie's doubly damned because Tony thinks she was Bryan's last squeeze and maybe now he can claim her like a sex scavenger. Somehow, though, I don't think she's that easy.

"Yo, Jul!" he shouts into the kitchen. "You'd better not be sayin' any shit about me in there."

I shout back. "We've got better things to discuss."

"Well, if I find out you said anything to her about me, I'll bust your face in!"

I softly tell Melanie, "Ignore him." But I can tell from her face that Tony's pissed her off big-time. *Don't,* I think, but it's too late. She charges into the living room to my imagined rescue, confronting Tony. "How can you talk to your wife that way?" Tony is stunned as she continues. "I heard about your beating Julie! You have no right to treat her that way!"

I think, *oh, shit!*

That's when Sue gets into the act. I hear her high-pitched squeal: "Who the hell are you to come into his house and tell him what to do?!"

That does it. Now Melanie's voice *projects;* I swear she's done theater. "And how the hell can *you* call yourself her *friend,* if you let Tony abuse her?! You should be ashamed of yourself!"

Sue's not my friend, and what happens next is priceless. She screams out: "That's it! I'm fuckin' leaving! I'll sleep in a ditch before I'll sleep with you again if I have to put up with this shit!" And she sneers at Tony. "I'm not going with no guy who can't control his women!"

Her included, I guess, as she storms out, slamming the front door. Then Carrie comes running into the kitchen to me, tears streaking down her face, Mike following her in.

I hold her as tight as a talisman. Greg tries to shepherd Melanie into the kitchen, mumbling about her dropping the fight, but Tony follows, goes to the counter and grabs a meat cleaver, facing her, hissing, "I'm gonna kill you, bitch! I'm gonna kill you, you mother fucker!"

I feel Bryan pushing me to the kitchen screen door. I escape outside with Carrie. The commotion in the kitchen goes on, voices filtering through, my heart thumping. I hear Melanie respond to Tony, her voice unbelievably steady and self-assured: "If you do, you'll go to jail and rot there for the rest of your life."

Mike tells me later what happened next, that Tony pulled back his hand and arm to throw the cleaver at Melanie, and shot his hand forward like he'd really let it fly at her. But in a split second, he twisted his aim and sent the cleaver crashing loudly into the sink. And Melanie didn't flinch. Almost as if she knew Tony wouldn't do it.

I finally deem it safe to come back in with Carrie. Melanie and Tony stand there, staring each other down, then he says, "You'd better watch your step, girl. I won't put up with your shit."

Melanie tells him, "And I won't put up with yours."

He glances at me and Carrie, then stomps out and up the stairs to lick his ego. I wonder where all this will lead me. *Can't be good,* I think.

* * * *

But it is, initially at least. Tony doesn't try to kick Melanie out of our lives. He hears her sing and play the guitar and decides she can join our group. He grudgingly accepts her.

Melanie has a friend, a hypnotherapist helping her quit smoking, named Frank. He's also helping get her musical career going, and he gets us a gig playing at a local high school prom. Tony's drumming is badly off and nearly ruins the gig, but the rest of us pull it off. Two boys come up to Melanie and me after the final set and tell us: "You girls are good, but you've got to lose that drummer." We nod; luckily Tony doesn't hear them.

* * * *

But Frank is of the same opinion and arranges a secret recording session for Melanie and me. I tell Tony I'm spending the weekend at Melanie's apartment to compose and work on new songs, taking Carrie with me. We do the session on Saturday afternoon. Frank holds the master tape to make duplicates and promote us and gives Melanie a duplicate for us.

I'm not crazy about Frank. He asks me to wear dark glasses to hide my eyes, but I refuse. I am what I am. He shrugs and doesn't press me further about it. Still, he's on our side, working with us for free, believing in our songs and career, so I don't mention this to Melanie.

I go back home. Melanie works as a secretary in downtown Philly during the week, and I have my kid to take care of, along with myself and Tony. I don't see how we're going to manage gigs that exclude Tony. The next night I hear him outside drinking with a neighbor. The neighbor tells Tony that I don't kowtow to him because Melanie's a bad influence on me. Tony comes in and starts raging about a locked keepsake box I have. I open it to show him the innocent crap inside: pictures of rock stars, old costume jewelry, childhood mementos. But it's not the answer he wanted; he wanted to find something incriminating. So he pushes me around and his fighting ends with him forcing me to do my so-called wifely duty. Afterwards he falls into a drunken sleep.

The next morning I get up early. Tony snores away. I decide to leave him. My sister Patty always said that Carrie and I were welcome to move in with her in Norwich, Connecticut, if I decided to split. But I need money for train tickets.

I stuff a suitcase with things for Carrie and me. Carrie seems more than willing to go on this adventure, grabbing her stuffed bear from her toys. We go to my parents' house to tell them and Tony, Jr. that we're leaving. I'm not deserting my son. I know he'll be safe with my parents. I ask my Mom and Dad for the train money. But my parents are tight that week. They support my decision to leave Tony, but they don't have cash. I use their phone to call Melanie at work. Melanie suggests we go to lunch and talk, worried that we should plan this a bit more. I tell her *no,* that *I'm leaving today.* Bryan was right about Melanie. She leaves work, grabs a cab to pick Carrie and me up and takes us to 30th Street Station, buying our tickets to put us on the train to Connecticut.

Patty has been called and is expecting us. Before we leave, Melanie maps out a plan for our future. She'll empty out her savings account, resign from her job and join us in New England, which has a thriving music scene where we can ply our talents. We'll both get day jobs and work up a folk repertoire in our spare time, singing and playing wherever we can on weeknights and weekends. Patty agrees to watch Carrie for us while we get settled in and established.

Carrie and I make our escape, a strange and exhilarating feeling as we board the train that Wednesday morning. Melanie waves goodbye from the platform, and Carrie asks as the train pulls out, "Are we going away for a long time, Mommy?"

"I hope so, honey. We're going to a new life."

I wonder how Tony will react when he wakes up in the early afternoon and finds us gone. I left no note. He doesn't deserve one. I try to psychically feel Bryan's presence, but he's not around. I sigh and watch the scenery blur past outside the train window.

* * * *

Everything is good the first two days at Patty's place. Even though my Mom tells Tony where Carrie and I have gone, he only seems concerned about seeing Carrie. Maybe it's the shock, my walking out on him so firmly, but on Friday, his true colors flare up again.

He tells my Mom he's taking me to court, that I crossed state lines with

Carrie, kidnapping her. Then he fires the one sure shot at me: he's going to take Tony, Jr. away from my parents. My father goes ballistic. My Mom calls me at Patty's, saying, "Get home and work it out."

Then Tony calls me to run his mouth about Melanie, how he'll take her to court for aiding me, giving me money. He goes on and on about our being lesbians, something he's decided despite its falsity. Melanie later tells me how he pulled a prank phone call on her, pretending he was from a social agency and wanted to talk about her "part in the kidnapping." Recognizing his voice, she played along, saying I was fleeing a vile, abusive husband. When she confronted Tony, he hung up on her.

But his threats about Tony, Jr. were real. Carrie and I take the train back to Philly on Monday. My father meets us at the station, taking us to his house, where Tony is waiting. He starts harassing me. "I stopped your blind pension check," he gloats, but he's lying and it comes on time.

That night Tony waits until Carrie's asleep. Mike and Greg go home, and I go upstairs to lay down and cradle my lost dream of freedom. But Tony comes in the bedroom, closes the door. He starts pushing me around, bruising me, muttering, "You're gonna leave me, huh? You're gonna leave me, huh?" over and over like a bitter mantra. I take it until his hands close around my throat, choking me hard. I fight back, trying to claw his hands away, panicking. I can't breathe. And behind Tony, I see Bryan. He's not transparent. Not ethereal. He's solid as a rock.

Bryan grabs Tony's hair, yanking him back, and Tony whirls around, not knowing who's attacking him, but ready to fight. And sees Bryan and freezes. "You're—You're—"

"I'm *back*," Bryan growls, "the prick *is in!*" He slugs Tony solidly in his face.

Tony touches his mouth and nose with his fingers and stares at the blood. "But you're *dead, man!*" He cringes, scuttling back on the mattress.

"Not as dead as *you'll be,* jerk, if you ever hurt Julie again. You understand, you little bastard?!"

"You're—you're—the prick!"

Bryan answers as coldly as the grave: "And I'll return to finish you off, if you ever beat Julie again."

I watch the stark fear on Tony's face as Bryan literally fades away. Tony, his face a smeared red mess, stumbles out of the bedroom. I hear the bathroom faucet running and, a few minutes later, Tony's steps going downstairs.

I turn out the light and get under the bed covers, pulling them tightly around me. I'm in shock, too. Bryan's materialization saved my life.

In the morning I find Tony on the living room couch with an ice bag on his nose and upper lip. He doesn't say one word about what happened, and

I don't either. But he never physically abuses me again.

* * * *

On Tuesday I call Melanie, telling her I'm back and what happened. She's also shocked, even more upset when I tell her Tony won't let me see her, that I'll call her when it's safe, when Tony's not around. A week later Tony relents enough to let us talk on the phone. She tells me Bryan is still around, and I say, he's still with me, too, probably guarding me from Tony.

When Melanie's former boyfriend, an army medic named Sal, comes home from Vietnam, he proposes and she accepts. She even tells him about Bryan, but I don't think he takes her seriously. Bryan decides that the marriage will keep the rest of his mortal competition away from Melanie and stands possessively at her other side when she takes her vows with Sal. And Tony decides that marriage will teach Melanie to toe a wifely line, and since she's invited us to the wedding, he lets me befriend her again.

When Melanie gets pregnant, Tony's twice as sure that she'll mend her feisty ways. He lets Carrie and me travel to Harrisburg, where Melanie now lives with Sal, finishing his army stint at Indian Town Gap. We visit them twice, once in late 1970 before the baby is born, and a second week in early 1971 after the baby comes. Sal lets Melanie name their son Bryan.

The ghostly Bryan dotes on his namesake, but Melanie still hasn't learned to keep her visions to herself. Neither take my advice, given as gently as I can, that some things aren't meant to be shared between the living and the dead. It's soon apparent that Sal doesn't believe in her ghost and tells her to live in the real world. I strongly suggest to Melanie that, where ethereal matters are concerned, we should *shut our mouths*. If she hadn't married Sal, our friendship would have died. And on the 1971 visit, we record our songs on a cassette tape recorder for the last time.

After Sal's discharge, they move back to Philadelphia. But their marriage fails. They divorce in 1973, and she and her son move in with her mother. We're still trying to get together musically, working with other back-up guys, then Tony finds a new way to vent his jealousy toward Melanie. He kills the dream that Melanie and I once shared and I can't let her know how.

If Tony ever carries out his final threat, it will hurt me far worse than his fists, and I know of only one way to make sure that never happens.

I try to let Melanie down easy, but she's tenacious, refusing to let the dream go. I finally tell her to live her own life without me.

She lashes back at me, unable to believe that I won't defy Tony. I tell her harshly, "You're the one who can't let the dead rest in peace. Well, you've got to give up *our* ghost. We have to let it go!"

I tell her to say goodbye. I become the coldest bitch in the world, a brick wall, and she finally stops banging her head against the end of our friendship.

"Well," she asks hopefully during our last phone call, "do you want me to call you every now and then, just to keep in touch?"

"I don't think so." I keep my voice carefully unemotional.

She's silent.

"Go on with your own life, Melanie."

Her voice echoes her disbelief. "Then I guess this is goodbye." Her tone says: *You're abandoning me.*

"I guess it is." My mind answers: *I am.*

She's silent again. Before she can argue further, I hang up the phone.

That's the last I hear from Melanie for 35 years.

Bryan comes around only once, upbraiding me for shutting Melanie out of my life. I quietly describe Tony's threat.

Bryan reacts with surprise, sadness and resignation. His spirit drifts away with a final echo: *I'll be back.*

Intuition tells me it won't be soon.

* * * *

From 1973 to June 2008, neither Melanie nor Bryan were in my life.

I clean up all the loose ends of that life and, with Carrie's moral support, divorce Tony in 1989. Carrie eventually has her own relationships and children, and when Melanie does find me and calls me in 2008, Carrie is a young grandmother and I'm a great-grandmother.

Melanie had two failed marriages, but her third one, to a history teacher named Tom of high intelligence and a kind nature, is still going strong after ten years. Her son Bryan, now 39, has married and divorced and has five children. Life moved on.

So did the ghostly Bryan. In 1975, Melanie's master spirit guide sent him away for 33 years for interfering with her mortal destiny. Bryan didn't take that well. He'd sneak around to see her a few times each year, pleading for a minute of her time, her other guides literally spiriting him away.

She didn't know that the powers-that-be had repressed her feelings for Bryan. His only hope was being told that one day he could return to her. And one day in late February, 2008, when he snuck around again, her current guide told them: *It's all right. Bryan can stay. It's time for you two to work things out.*

Her husband Tom doesn't really care if she believes in ghosts, as long as she keeps them out of his way, since *he doesn't* believe in them. Bryan also changed, maturing in the afterlife.

* * * *

In March 2008, going through her keepsakes, Melanie found our old letters, cassettes and tapes, things we shared so many years ago. She wanted to find me, but I'd long since moved to Illinois, following my parents and Patty out here. Carrie lived just outside of Philly with her husband and three younger daughters, and Tony, Jr. lived with his wife and children in Tennessee. Time scattered us. And Tony had died two years ago, succumbing to cancer. I didn't weep, only hoped his spirit would rectify his mistakes the next time around, if he got a second chance.

Tom helped Melanie to locate me through the Internet; luckily, I have a somewhat unusual full name: Julianna Marguerite Castevella. They found my phone number in Illinois, and in the first week of June, about a week before my birthday, she called me. And said: "Dear sister, please forgive me for not trying to find you earlier."

I'm not her blood sister, but she meant every word. I told her I was the one who disappeared. She didn't owe me forgiveness, but I welcomed the return of our friendship.

We talked and talked and talked. Every week. And I traveled back to Philly for Christmas and New Year's Eve 2008, spending the first week with Carrie and her family and most of the second week with Melanie and Tom...and with a ghost named Bryan.

He helps Melanie with her music and other projects, is a spiritual companion to her, and occasionally to me, in our golden years. She still wants to make music with me, but, unfortunately, we're numerous states apart. For now, she's learning how to work a computerized recording studio. We practiced our old songs during my visit and later swapped music through the mail. We're not going to find fame and fortune in our early sixties, but we'll have whatever life allows in the time left to us.

Melanie never asked me why I shut her out of my life so firmly in 1973. She told me she finally accepted it as a choice I made, whether she understood it or not.

I reluctantly told her the truth during one of our lengthy Sunday afternoon phone calls. "You never knew this, but Tony had connections to the mob. He threatened to have you killed, either doing it himself or paying some low life as nasty as he was to do it." I didn't describe Tony's full scenario to her. Some nightmares are best forgotten.

"You were protecting me."

"Yes. I couldn't be certain he wouldn't follow through on that threat. I worried that one day you'd be attacked or worse. I did feel bad about what happened after I returned from Connecticut. But Melanie, no matter what we tried for, Tony would have wrecked it. And I couldn't break away from him then."

"And now he's dead." I heard an edge of satisfaction in her voice that

I understood.

"Yeah, funny, isn't it? Some people like Bryan return, but we hope some like Tony never return."

"Good riddance to bad rubbish."

"I'll second that thought."

She stayed quiet for a moment, then: "Thank you for making that sacrifice, Julie. For protecting me from Tony, from my own hard-headed self, even when it meant ending our friendship."

"I had to say goodbye, to make sure he'd leave you alone. I knew you'd be all right, that you'd find your own way eventually." I sensed Bryan beside me. He whispered telepathically to me. I smirked. "Bryan's here. He says that when we reach the afterlife, where we'll be, Tony can't follow."

I can feel her grin on her face as she says *"Good!"*

Life surprised us in the end. Our friendship survived. Melanie and Tom are planning to visit me soon in Illinois. Bryan will probably tag along too, standing in the shadows.

SEASTRUCK

"I don't paint fantasy anymore," Mary told the interviewer, when he had asked about the portrait of Poseidon hanging in the corner of her third-floor studio. "It's simply that real life has more compelling subjects." But after he had left, she went back upstairs to the portrait and stared at it. The memories hurt, as they came flooding back to her.

She recalled that long ago, cloudless, late summer evening, when she'd moved into the beach house in Monterey. Her grandmother had bequeathed the two-story cottage to Mary, along with a modest trust fund, a godsend that allowed her to paint fulltime and build a career in the fine arts. Moonlight through the picture windows had illuminated the bedroom and living room as she unpacked, the sturdy cottage fitting her belongings like a charm.

She unpacked her art supplies last, putting them in the small enclosed porch, glassed in and facing west, north and east.

It was well past midnight when she carried the boxes, flattened and bundled, out back, stacking them against the house. Then she went inside and stood in the living room, gazing through its picture window at the equal blackness of sea and sky. Beyond the dunes fronting her property, the sound of the surf pounding the shore made her sleepy.

She pleasantly collapsed on her roomy sofa and woke up the next morning on it, with a picture in her mind of the sea and sky and a tall, arrogant man standing on the wet shore, his back to the ocean.

A sort of Poseidon, but youthful. Beardless, with muscles smooth and ungnarled, his wet dark hair sculpted against his head and neck, his eyes commanding and shrewd.

The idea intrigued her. She ate a quick breakfast, put a clean canvas on the easel and began to paint it.

Three days later, as grey afternoon light from an overcast sky threw muted shadows about her new home, she finished the painting.

She decided to walk on the beach for exercise. Locking up, she walked down the wooden backstairs, went around her house and stepped onto the silvered dusky sand. Grey waves and white surf rushed the shoreline. No rain yet, but it was coming.

Her light blue Windbreaker over her shorts and top offered some warmth against the cool sea wind, and her sandals dug into the sand. She climbed over the sparse dunes and emerged on the shore, awed by the turbulent ocean, the impending storm.

The dunes to her left receded and withdrew into wild scrub along the coastal highway. The beach expanded as she walked, a wide swath between scrub and sea. Wave caps, frothing, swept their white tendrils out, serrated like miniature claws, to grasp the wet rim of the shore. The clouds, above the choppy swells, roiled grey and black, moving fast.

The storm suddenly felt unclean and corrupting. The frail human form held no protection against such a wild elemental dance. She turned back, heading to the safety of her house.

Rain began pattering down as she hurried on, eyes drawn to the angry sea. Then she saw the swimmer, floating on the far waves.

Her heart quickened, for who would venture out into the ocean in such weather? Some unfortunate soul, pulled down into the rough undertow by the unforeseen storm? A corpse?

But, no. Mary detected movement, an arm lifting, arcing, plowing back down into the water. A swimmer, very much alive, his every stroke controlled and self-assured. And making excellent headway, moving to shore.

The rain fell more heavily, and the swimmer reached standable bottom and straightened up. A man. He walked toward her, toward where she stood on the sodden beach.

Instinct told her to flee from a stranger emerging from a storm-tossed sea, but if the man needed medical attention or simple human assistance, running away was unthinkable.

She waited, ready to help, but also ready to flee if he threatened her.

The man stopped a few feet from her, studying her as she studied him. His face was solemn with sharply angular features framed by thick black hair, wet and tangled against his neck and shoulders. Much taller than her, his naked, muscled body gleamed in the heavy downpour, his genitals cupped but not covered by a rope made of seaweed.

That alone made her back up, fearful, when she noticed gills protruding from each side of his neck and torso, expanding with the man's exerted breathing, filmy and light grey against brown skin flaps partially covering them. Her eyes, straining in her shock, met his.

His own dark eyes placidly studied her, his face chiseled, immobile. He made no move to harm her but her brain rebelled against the sight of a living merman, and she blacked out.

She came to in her house, stretched out on the living room sofa, encrusted and gritty sand on her skin and clothes and in her hair. She got nervously to her feet and slid her hand into her pocket. Her keys were missing.

She moved silently to the kitchen and switched on the light to see small scatterings of sand on the linoleum floor and the side door unlocked and ajar and her keys on the kitchen table.

She relocked the side door and returned to the darkening living room, switching on a lamp and glancing at the wall clock. Nearly seven p.m. How long had it been since she'd fainted on the shore? Had the merman found her keys and carried her home?

The storm still battered the coast, rain sheeting down. The house remained quiet. She grasped a pair of scissors from her art cabinet, slowly climbed the carpeted staircase to the second floor, and cautiously flicked on the lights: no one in her bedroom, bathroom or guest room, no water stains nor sand marring the rugs or linoleum.

She caught her reflection in the bathroom mirror, her long blonde hair tangled in gritty knots, her hazel eyes dark-circled, and her face and neck as spotted and streaked with dried grey sand as the rest of her.

She went back downstairs, making sure the front door was still locked and double-bolted, rechecking the locks on the side door.

Her artist's nook, the enclosed porch, was a side extension, one step down to the left of her living room, crowded with her cabinet, rattan chair, artist's stool and easel and the finished portrait of Poseidon. Yes, the face on the canvas was strangely similar to the merman's. Had she imagined his gills, the rain and the poor light creating that illusion? Heightened by her painting? The mind could play very believable tricks.

She put the question aside and went up to shower the grit off her body. Then she slept until morning, got dressed and ate, and walked along the beach to where the man had emerged from the waves to find both shore and ocean undisturbed. She went home and busied herself. She gave up trying to understand and hoped it was an isolated, strange event of the type that never repeats itself.

When night returned, she unlocked her kitchen side door, hauling out another bag of trash. A multitude of stars shone above her, and she sat on the steps, leaning against the wooden railing, looking up at them.

She massaged her neck, shutting her eyes momentarily at the pleasure. When she opened them, he moved silently out of the shadowed dunes and stood in the small beam of light coming from her kitchen. He did have gills, expanding and contracting rapidly. Fear knotted her stomach and prickled her skin. He held an enormous conch shell, symmetrically perfect, sea-scoured, its inner whorl glazed with a pearl-like sheen. He edged to her, offering it.

"Who are you?" she whispered. *"What* are you?"

He pointed silently to himself, moved past the house, pointed toward the sea, then touched his chest once more.

"You're from the sea?" she asked nervously. The question sounded inane.

He nodded his head once, solemnly.

"You can understand me. Can you speak?"

Moving past her, he skimmed up her side steps. Cradling the shell against him, he opened the screen door and beckoned to her. From his mouth came an incomprehensible barrage of clicks and whistles that seemed to fade in pitch as he uttered them.

She shook her head and gestured that he should remain outside. She had to make him come back, to somehow get herself inside the house and lock the door and call the police and *not* tell them about his gills. She hoped that the authorities wouldn't hurt him, but there were no other options. Let the scientists figure him out after she was safely inside.

The merman waited for her at the half-opened screen door. Mary pointed to where she stood, shook her head firmly again and gestured once more that he should come back down the steps. In response, he simply walked into her house. The screen door clattered and closed.

Mary stood there, her first impulse to get in her car and drive to the police, and then she remembered her keys were in her handbag in the living room. Running seemed pointless. He could catch her before she made it to another house further up the coast.

She took deep breaths, devising a plan. She would go in, smile politely and rummage through the handbag. *Put on lipstick,* she thought, *comb your hair. It must look natural. Then make an excuse to go to the car, get in and lock the doors and drive to the police station.*

She followed him in to the living room. He stood by the breakfront that faced her living room windows and, beyond them, the ocean. Her handbag sat on the breakfront's sleek, cherrywood surface, and the stunning conch shell sat beside it. The polished wood cast darkly mirrored reflections, of the shell and of him and of her as she came up beside him and traced the lines of the shell with her fingers. The merman's hand reached out, covering hers as it covered the shell. Then he released her, moving away.

A sharp, burning tingle spread across her hands. She examined them, but found no mark, no reason for their discomfort.

Then a twinge of vertigo struck her. She clutched at the breakfront to steady herself.

The merman now stood on the porch, staring at her portrait of Poseidon. He turned to look at her, smiling, pleased.

Her dizziness and discomfort in her hands abruptly stopped. She was suddenly unafraid. He meant her no harm. He had brought her a gift. "Yes, it looks very much like you."

He answered in his warbling tongue.

"I'm sorry. I don't understand your language."

He pointed to his sides and neck and then to the costumed figure in the painting.

"Oh, no gills."

He nodded.

"It's supposed to be Poseidon, a god. Do you even know who Poseidon was?"

He gave her another singular, serious nod.

"You do? How did you learn about…" (she almost said "mortal") "… my culture? My language?"

His hands rose, long-fingered, to touch his ears, then his eyes (which held a condescending but not unpleasant mirth). And then, surprisingly, his forehead.

"You hear, you see, you think."

He smiled.

"I've never seen a human with gills. Nor wearing a seaweed jockstrap. You know that science would say that your anatomy isn't possible. The gills, I mean."

His smile widened and gave way to a careless amiable laugh. He came over to her and took her hand in his.

Laughter is a human attribute, Mary thought, and waited for his next attempt to communicate. He drew their clasped hands to rest once more against the shell. Again, the vertigo hit her, but he pressed his arm against her back, held her and drew her against him, lowering his face to her own. She tried to pull away, but his embrace tightened. An intense desire totally foreign to her nature overwhelmed her. As she met his kiss, words swirled in her mind: <Now you are mine.>

He pulled her to the rug, their bodies flaring, uniting, utterly fulfilling themselves. In the afterglow, his fingers gently explored her, stroking her delicately. As she started slipping off to sleep, he carried her up to her bed.

When she awoke alone in the pre-dawn hours, the absurdity of it all frightened her, as if she were caught in a dream; the worst of it was finding herself in love with him. A man whose eyes, momentarily locking with hers, had mentally warned her to keep his existence secret. A man whose name she didn't yet know and whose culture she couldn't comprehend. A man who shouldn't—couldn't—logically exist.

She went downstairs and lightly traced the sleek whorls of the shell with her fingers. The tingling returned, reminding her of his touch.

The next night she waited for him, and he returned.

Her fingers brushed his dampened hair, and she thought, *Is this madness?*

A scratching answer whispered inside her head, forming words in English, like a worn phonograph record played at low volume, yet so alien in tone, that she backed away. His nonverbal laughter crackled like the buzz of insects against her inner ear. <Hear me, Mary. I am speaking through what your people label telepathy.>

She tried thinking a response, but his telepathic voice interrupted, startling her with its sudden clarity and its subtle strangeness. <Do not force it. I can pick up your natural thoughts, but when you strain to control them, they become garbled. Speak verbally, and I will answer you telepathically. I am not what you first supposed me to be: a mentally deficient hybrid with no knowledge of your world and its culture.>

She blushed, although he really shouldn't have faulted her for that, then quietly and carefully sent him a mental question: <What's your name?!>

He smiled and sent a responding thought. <Hayja.>

She tried it aloud. "Hade…cha. Hade-cha?"

<Eliminate the 'd' and the 'ch' and replace them with a 'y' and a 'j.'>

"Hayja."

He nodded approvingly. <My own language is beyond your human diction, but I can speak telepathic English and other tongues fluently.>

"Hayja…your gills…if you're not human, then what are you?"

He hesitated, studying her, then said, <If I tell you I am a god, and have traveled far to answer a silent song you sang, will you believe me?>

Mary shook her head. "We obviously share the same genus. Perhaps our species differ, but I don't believe in gods from the sea."

He shrugged. <If it pleases you, I will strive to explain in a manner you can comprehend. My people can inhabit the sea, but are also amphibious and can surface without difficulty.>

"Well, you look human, outside of your gills. Not to mention sexual compatibility." She colored slightly. He grinned and stroked her cheek, but she persisted. "But why are your people undiscovered? Another human species co-existing among mankind?"

<The attempts by my people to communicate with yours were met with fear, aggression and ignorance. We chose to hide ourselves from humans, except for those we wished to reveal ourselves to. To those so blessed, we were a gift, they believed, from the gods. But our respective people are not irreconcilably different, as you've found out, becoming my mate.>

"Your mate?"

<We are mated,> he said simply. <You accepted my gifts, both of them, last night without challenge or denial.>

"Both gifts? There was only the conch shell…" She blushed.

He spoke aloud in his language, a melodious whistle with two clicks, then explained telepathically, <In your tongue, this would mean mingling the soul or essence of oneself with another's soul or essence. The shell was the conductor as we touched it. Our mating completed it.>

"I'm not a child, Hayja. I'm 24, young enough to believe that strange things can occur, but old enough to know that they happen for a logical reason. That shell can't overwhelm me with emotions and make me lose control the way I did last night. It was all sudden and frightening, but somehow I trust you. And, yes, love you. But it makes no sense, and until we understand what's happening, we should slow this thing down. It's too soon to talk of being mated."

He simply reached for her and drew her to him, and her own acquiescence, her eagerness, betrayed her argument and silently but eloquently answered him.

Her dual life began then. He appeared each night like a recurring dream and left her before morning came.

She installed a strong, outdoor light under the roof that jutted off her enclosed studio porch. At night, she turned it on, illuminating a stretch of the dunes beyond the louvered porch windows, and locked her doors. As she worked at her easel, she watched for Hayja's arrival through the screen behind the glass panes, then let him in, soaking her brushes, letting the canvas dry until the next day.

Sometimes they talked in their strange way. Other times few words were said before they made love. Afterwards, satiated, she would drift to sleep beside him. Morning always found him gone and her house securely relocked.

When she went out for food and other supplies, she kept to herself and made no new friends, something very unlike her. She worried about unexpected visitors, but Hayja quieted her fears, insisting he could *sense* the approach of landfolk and avoid them.

Sometimes he would tell her he was going away and return to the sea for unexplained reasons. She missed him bitterly. She would pace the beach like a deprived addict and plunge into the waves, searching the ocean's horizon.

When he came back to her, she questioned him, and his answers were curt and dismissive.

What did he eat?

<The bounty of the gods,> he laughed, and refused to eat her food.

Where did his people dwell in the ocean? He answered her brusquely: <Places you have no access to.>

When she researched sea mammals in the local library and asked Hayja how they might relate to his people, he glared at her, strode tautly from her house and didn't return for a week.

She began to rethink her intense desire and love for Hayja, new and unpleasant emotions rising inside her, demanding her attention. If Hayja felt the fear and doubt building in her mind, felt his glamorous hold on her weaken, he gave no sign of it.

Three months passed since they first met on the storm-blasted beach.

Now December winds buffeted the California coastline, and Hayja would appear on two, perhaps three nights each week, seduce her to their mutual satisfaction and make light of her fears when she spoke of them.

He laid down rules for her to follow as his mate. She must live as if celibate and never betray his presence to other landfolk. She could do her work and develop careful friendships and even travel if she forewarned him. But he demanded both loyalty and secrecy from her. She had accepted his mating gift and mated with him. She must adjust her life to his needs and not dishonor him.

He couldn't conceive of her inability to live such a dual life and her rejection of the hidden and the unknown, which he now represented to her. It broke the spell, made her see him with clear, frightened eyes. She knew that the onus was on her to end their relationship with love and regret, without damaging Hayja's pride or endangering herself or him. If they went on like this, humanity would eventually discover him, prod and measure him like a freak. He must willingly return to the sea and his own world.

She took up the challenge, actively courting the Monterey and Carmel art galleries, creating and selling her paintings with renewed vigor. She branched cautiously into a social night life among the local talent, feeding Hayja excuses about building professional contacts when he grumbled. If she broke his rules, perhaps he would leave her. She had to end this for both their sakes.

An exclusive salon in Carmel ran a one-woman show of her work, and during the evening opening, she met highly respected members of Southern California's literary and art communities. Among them was Daniel Forbes.

Patricia, the gallery owner, introduced them. "Mary, this is Daniel Forbes. He's trying to hide it, but he turned 30 today and he's feeling like an old codger. Cheer him up, won't you, with your youth and vitality?"

With a prodding touch on Mary's arm, Patricia disappeared into the crowd. Mary stood there, trying to think up something to say, staring at Daniel, a pleasant looking man with a lopsided smile. He beat her to it. "Now don't go telling anyone else I hail from the age of dinosaurs!" He widened his eyes, bright and mischievous, with a lift of his brows, and pursed his lips for emphasis.

His relaxed demeanor made her smile. He had curly blonde hair, was rugged in features and build. While aesthetically handsome, Daniel's face showed nothing of the masterful, neither demanding nor explicit. It reflected warmth, humor and the pleasure of possibilities.

"If you're a dinosaur," she said, "then you must have ages of wisdom stored in your head."

"Nope," he said, "my brain, I hear, is the size of a peanut. Shrunk when

I woke up this morning." His brown eyes twinkled and his mouth stretched, grinning with mirth.

"Then you can't be a dinosaur," Mary said. "Wit, they say, stems from intelligence. Judging from that, I'd say your brain expanded, rather than shrank, this morning."

"Well, thank you for the compliment." He made a mock bow.

"Happy Birthday," Mary said.

They spent the remainder of the evening together. Daniel critiqued her paintings. He was an art critic for various local newspapers, an art historian with three well-received biographies to his credit, and earned a further living appraising, repairing and restoring art and antiques. His knowledge spanned from the ancient to the modern world.

She enjoyed his commentary tremendously, but when he offered to follow her home for a night cap, she declined, fearing that Hayja would appear, sensing her attraction for Daniel as a shark senses blood. But Hayja never showed that night or any other night that week.

Relieved but lonely, when Daniel called to suggest dinner the following Friday, she accepted.

They ate at a small Italian bistro in Monterey then strolled along Cannery Row. It was late when Daniel pulled his Rambler alongside Mary's covered station wagon and waited, silently handing her the reins of their budding relationship.

She felt the tension between them, found her courage and asked Daniel in for a drink. They sat in her living room, talking over their liquors, but her eyes kept straying to Hayja's portrait, now framed and prominently displayed. Her guilt and confusion pushed against the emotional dam she had built. Her eyes brimmed with tears. Wiping them away, she apologized, but when Daniel hugged her and stroked her hair, the dam broke. He let her cry it out, comforting her, kissing her face gently. At some point, she kissed him back. Their passion flared, but before it ignited, Daniel pulled away and gallantly offered to stop if she thought he was rushing her. Mary said three words: "I need you," and knew he couldn't understand the fuller meaning behind them: her need to be touched and loved by one of her own people. How could he know?

Later that night, Mary fell asleep with Daniel's arms wrapped protectively around her, snugly embraced by a man who walked her own world.

She dreamt that Daniel and Hayja stood glaring at one another, and then she awoke, saw Daniel still asleep beside her and the sea man standing beside the bed, glaring down at him, eyes alight with fury. Hayja slowly turned his gaze to her, where she cowered beneath the covers. He sent a telepathic warning into her mind and left her bedroom so silently, that in the morning she wondered if it'd been part of her dream. But she took no further chances. She made Daniel a quick breakfast and sent him on his way over his protests, saying she had a project to complete.

Daniel called her twice that day, concerned for her. She kept the conversation short, assuring him she was fine, and, yes, she cared for him, but needed to get back to her work. She spent a restless night, attempting to start a new painting, waiting for Hayja, imagining a dozen bad scenarios, and finally fell asleep undisturbed till morning.

The next day she let her answering machine pick up her calls and ignored Daniel's messages. She hardly ate or drank, her stomach queasy with nervousness, gearing up her courage to confront Hayja.

At sunset, she stood alone on the dunes, brilliant mauves, pinks and yellow-oranges coating the skies and casting kaleidoscope colors onto the sea. *I started this,* she thought. *Let me finish it with Daniel kept well out of it. Let Hayja vent his wrath on me.*

She feared him despite the love she still felt for him, a useless love that would isolate and destroy her and alienate them both. A love with no future.

The sunset faded. The wind off the sea blew colder and she zipped her jacket up, the sweatshirt under it and her bluejeans inadequate against the chill.

A starless night came on, promising rain. The clouds parted to reveal a full moon, then swallowed it again.

She caught a movement to her left. Hayja stood there, watching her.

<You have sent him away?> Hayja's question presupposed its answer. She faltered. "Not permanently."

He lightly caressed her cheek. <Why do you want to anger me?>

"I don't, but you refuse to listen to reason. I can't be your mate. We come from two different worlds. This *mating* should never have occurred." She fumbled, losing her bravery. "Why would you even want me as your mate?"

He gaped at her, unabashed surprise on his face. <Because I loved you. I heard your heart-song as you painted your canvas. It sang of Poseidon, of your love for the sea.>

"And you answered, subconsciously, with your own image."

His telepathic voice lowered, conveying subtle shades of arousal and honesty. <I sent you more than my image. I sent you my soul, my essence, which you accepted not only to complete your painting, but to complete the man who sent them to you. This is an honor among my people, a sacred gift which, once accepted, must be reciprocated in kind.>

"But I didn't ask for that gift. Not consciously, Hayja. You can't share my world, and I certainly know nothing of your people or their customs." Her voice rose, harsh against the rumble of the ocean.

<Why do you always ask of my kin? They exist beyond your reach

and understanding, yet I never fault you for this. Why then fault me for not exposing myself and my kin to be mocked once again by your people? We have the nights to share our separate worlds.>

"Sex isn't everything." Her words heated the cold night; her anger overrode her fear. "Men and women form relationships, sharing their lives and interests, and evolve beyond the physical."

<You can bond with your kind without mating with them. I give you ample time, when I travel the seas, for you to satisfy those needs. But I warn you again, I can sense your presence and that of others at great distances. I was with you last night as that man usurped my rightful place.>

"Did you gain anything by spying on me? Did you feel Daniel make love to me, feel how much he cared for me, beyond mere sexual attraction, beyond mere biological urge?"

He stiffened. <You have wronged me, and now you insult my feelings for you, as if I did not care for you beyond our joining.>

"Hayja, please...you need a woman from your own species. Interspecies either can't breed or produce sterile hybrids. If I become pregnant, how would I explain it and what would I bear?"

His face softened. <Is that what you fear, Mary? If you bore me a child, it could procreate again, but with a human like yourself. My species, as you call my people, became sterile. We faced extinction, before we discovered that we could procreate with your people. The children born of these unions are always the progeny of my kin. That is why we choose human mates. When I impregnate you, you will isolate yourself until the child is born. After its birth, I will take it to be raised among my people. You are our hope, Mary, and I chose you as my mate because you are beautiful, within and without, and worthy of my love. I know of this other love you speak of, this man's paltry affection, a bud often crushed before it can flower. What we have embarked on requires courage but I will never abandon you because of feckless emotions waxing and waning like the moon.>

Although his eloquence tore at her, she shook her head.

<Enough. Let us go in now. It is too cold for you on the beach.> He smiled and reached for her.

She drew back. "No."

<You are angering me.>

"Hayja, we have a phrase: letting go with love. Can you do it? Let me go with love? I can't have your child. I can't be your mate. What we've shared must end tonight. I'm sorry if this hurts you, but I belong with my own kind."

He winced at her words. <Honor demands that I offer leniency, if you correct this waywardness. You have one turn of the moon to end your relationship with Daniel and to accept your destiny with me. You mustn't test

my patience further after I return.>

He turned away, striding back into the sea.

"Hayja, please! Let me go! I can't do what you ask! This isn't my destiny!"

Hayja had submerged beneath the black waves.

* * * *

The month passed quickly, the moon turning full again. It vied with the stars, shedding clear light. Hayja climbed to where she stood on the sparse dunes. He once more demanded her fidelity. Mary again pleaded for her freedom. She had avoided letting Daniel visit her at home, making careful excuses, spending New Year's Eve at his apartment in Carmel, hoping to make Hayja see reason.

Now he vehemently refused, lividly swearing to teach her humility as his mate. She angrily countered that he couldn't force her to love him. He regarded her rigidly and coldly vowed to make her bow down before him as she would to a god.

Then he told her curtly that he would not lay hands upon her or stop her from seeing Daniel and laughed at her sudden confusion. <I am not giving you what you ask of me. My telepathic powers are greater than you could ever comprehend. I will simply eliminate my rival by forcing you to kill him.>

She watched as he left her imperiously, returning to the sea. Speechless and horrified, she slowly walked home, remembering his eyes as he issued his threat, reflecting his jealousy and determination.

For three weeks, Mary resisted Hayja's telepathic commands and kept Daniel, unaware of it, out of the battle. In the fourth week, Hayja's link became stronger, sending her messages of her defeat, of Daniel's death. She struggled against the images Hayja placed in her mind, of his victory over her, of her submission to him.

At January's end, the strain of the battle overwhelmed her.

She had stayed overnight that Friday at Daniel's apartment. On Saturday morning, they drove back to her beach house in her station wagon to pick up finished paintings to deliver to her gallery in Carmel on Monday. Mary insisted that they return to Carmel by early Saturday evening. She had made reservations at a restaurant there for a romantic dinner and planned to stay over Daniel's place until Monday.

She had made so many excuses to avoid Daniel's staying over at her house, he began teasing her about it. "Do you have another lover? A silkie from the sea?"

The question jolted her; she was glad her face was hidden as she bent over her paintings, stacked against the wall. "Don't be silly. It's more convenient to stay with you this weekend."

"And the last three weekends, too? I've been wondering why you don't want me around here at night. I mean, we've only been dating, going together, a few months, and maybe I have let things happen too fast, but it's real for me. I do love you. And it feels like you're shutting me out of a part of your life."

She straightened up and faced him. "I think I love you, too, Daniel. I just need some privacy to work on things. I might not get any work done, if you were around," she joked. "Give me some time, a little more, to get it together. Now help me take these paintings to the car. When we're done, I'll reward you. I'm in the mood."

They carried her artwork to the station wagon, arranging the canvases carefully in the back, then pulled a dark tarp over them to protect them from the sun, locked the car and went back inside.

He put his arms around her and lowered his mouth to hers. His kiss aroused her. She would tell him tomorrow about her plans to sell the house and move. The farther away from Hayja and the sea, the better. The gallery in Carmel wasn't her only stop in Carmel on Monday.

Hayja never came to her in bright daylight, never risked exposing himself to humans. "I want you," she told Daniel. "Right now."

"Isn't it a little early?" His hands contradicted him.

"It's never too early." She led him upstairs.

They took it slowly, making love for nearly two hours, and fell asleep afterwards.

Mary woke first, stretching languorously, late afternoon sun stealing through the slats of her bedroom blinds. She shut her eyes, catching a few minutes more rest, her mind drifting off pleasantly.

Then Hayja's voice shouted inside her head: <Kill him!> She tried to come awake again, but her body stayed asleep. It felt as if Hayja was invading it, seeping into her. Her eyes opened, and she quietly got up, leaving Daniel undisturbed. She trod softly down to the kitchen, both excited and repulsed by the thought of violence.

She carefully opened a drawer and chose a large sharp carving knife. Her hand faltered as she held it, and then the urge to kill came back into her, swirling inside of her intensely. *How good it would be to see the blood, to feel the flesh give way, as she plunged the knife into Daniel. How much pleasure there would be as she carved and sliced bits of him out, exposing those wonderous organs he kept hidden within.* Hayja's voice interrupted her mad thoughts, telling her where to stab first to kill Daniel instantly, and added: <Then you can play to your heart's desire with his remains.> She nodded to herself and slowly climbed the stairs and entered the bedroom.

Daniel had turned over, his back to her. Mary crept over to him, holding the knife in her fist, point downward. A portion of her sane self screamed at her, but Hayja's voice intruded: <It will feel so good to plunge it in. You know you want to kill him!>

Her hand lifted, taking aim.

And Daniel turned in his sleep, showing her the profile she so loved, when she awoke beside him in the night or in the morning. Her sanity broke through, rising from the dark violence Hayja had entrapped it in. She felt him try to force her hand down, to stab Daniel, but she ran from the room, ran downstairs to the kitchen and put the knife away. And cursed at Hayja, cursed him in her mind, that he wanted a womb and called it a woman, that he called this love, but he gave her no right to accept this or to refuse it. As if her life had little value outside of his needs, and the life of anyone else standing in his way had none.

Go away! she screamed at him, *go away and never come back!* Then she went upstairs, trembling from the shock of what she had nearly done, her naked body chilled, and woke Daniel up as tears flooded down her face.

Daniel gazed drowsily at her, then opened his eyes fully, sitting up and pulling her to him. "Mary, you're shaking. What's wrong?"

"I have to tell you something horrible. You may not believe me."

He pulled the covers over her, warming her. "Don't worry about that now. Just tell me."

Mary nodded. She told him about Hayja.

Daniel listened patiently, his eyes widening as Mary told him how she'd nearly murdered him that afternoon. Then he slowly got up and began to dress.

She watched him anxiously. "Are you angry, Daniel? Do you hate me?"

"No and no. Worried, yes. This guy's been playing with your mind, a pretty warped game at that. Get your clothes on. We're going to talk this out rationally. One thing you should notice is this man uttered this questionable threat one month ago, and during that entire month, you've never acted hostilely towards me until today. Why did Hayja wait this long before acting on his threat? Are his so-called powers fraudulent, is their only validity your belief in them?"

Mary dressed and followed him down to the living room. He examined the conch, then sat beside her on the couch.

Daniel spoke firmly. "Hayja's resemblance to Poseidon in your fantasy painting is mere coincidence, Mary, and I've held that conch shell from every angle without any physiological effect. Why doesn't this Hayja attack me directly? Why make you to do his dirty work?"

"He said your death by my hand would humiliate me and humble me to his will. I've been struggling to resist his will. This is the first time you've seen it, Daniel. He nearly succeeded twice before."

"Twice? I don't seriously believe, no matter what you tell me, that you want to kill me. But what happened before this?"

She hesitated, fearing it would drive him away, leaving her alone, but at least that would keep him safe.

She took his hand, squeezing it, afraid. "Please forgive me for this. Please. The night I dropped your full tea cup, breaking it on the kitchen floor? I'd put poison into it, powdered cleanser."

"The taste would have alerted me. But I could have induced vomiting and gotten myself to a hospital." He shuddered, but his voice sounded skeptical. "Now I'm more worried about you than this Hayja with his elaborate hoax, gills and all. What about the other time?"

Mary sighed. He had never seen Hayja, those gills expanding. "Two weeks ago, during that drive to Encino for that concert, when we turned that curve and I fell against you. He wanted me to grab the wheel, to crash the car into oncoming traffic."

"That endangers you. Why destroy his prize along with his rival?"

"He insisted he'd protect me from harm. He was watching the traffic through my eyes and trying to control my movements to make the impact occur only on the driver's side. Your side."

"That's not guaranteed," Daniel said softly.

"I didn't believe it either. What's more, if we hit another car, the people in it would also suffer. I couldn't bear that, and it broke his spell. I couldn't hurt you. I couldn't hurt others."

"The ego over the id. Morals and ethics over impulse."

"You can call it what you want, Daniel, if we both get out of this with our skins intact."

"We will," Daniel assured her. "What's important is that you're not giving in to these impulses."

She turned away from him, staring nervously through the picture window to the dunes and sea, now colored by the fading sunset. "If you don't believe Hayja is real and can do what I've told you, then you must think I'm criminally insane."

He didn't answer for a minute, just looked at her, and then he stroked her hair slowly. "Some people can be *compelling,* Mary. They set up a persona for themselves, so convincing, that others buy into it as if it were real. It's like being hypnotized, a magician's trick. That's what I think he's done to you."

She shook her head. "That doesn't excuse what I nearly did to you today. I can't believe I ever thought I loved him or that Hayja loved me. It seemed more a tangled desire we were caught up in."

"And I'm having a hard time believing that you really tried to knife me today, Mary. It sounds more like a waking dream, your mind playing tricks on you. That's first-degree murder, and it certainly wouldn't suit Hayja's plans to have you arrested, convicted and put away for my death. I think this man's trying to drive you insane for his own sick reasons. I certainly wouldn't call that love."

She shook her head again and held his gaze without flinching. "Every night last week he sent me images of how he'd accomplish your death through me, spoke to me through my mind. Remember that your car isn't here, that we're driving back to Carmel in mine today. Hayja intended to destroy your corpse, to take it out to sea, to make it look as if you'd simply disappeared. He said he could wipe the memory of your death from my mind, make me believe that I was innocent of it, that you were really missing. He screamed at me, both in English and in his strange, whistling language. My head felt as if it would tear apart. He said that if I failed, he would defend his own honor, that if you returned here, he would know it and kill you himself. That's why we can't stay here, Daniel. We have to go *now.*"

Daniel stared at her for what seemed too long a time, then he slowly stood up. "We'll leave. He's obviously dangerous, but whatever his game, he's not a merman. If such creatures existed, science would have found evidence of it. If his species became sterile, his people would die out quickly, despite his bull about humans bearing their children. If they're born, they also eventually die. Where are the bodies? When bodies decay, they bloat up with gas. They float, get washed to shore."

"Or get eaten."

Daniel winced. "There are no merpeople, Mary. Subs and research vessels cruise the ocean depths for decades now. Not one shred of proof exists for an amphibious human species. And no species has disposed of its dead without a trace, without a single slip-up through the centuries. Hayja is lying, and we're going to find out what his real game is, but not tonight and not alone. You'll stay with me, Mary, away from here, until we figure out how to expose him and stop his game. You may not be the only woman he's playing merman with, but we'll make sure you're the last."

Mary stood up and hugged him tightly. "Thank you for believing me, for not thinking I was crazy."

He hugged her back. "Run upstairs and pack an overnight bag. We can come back tomorrow for anything else you want, but we'll bring some friends along for back-up. I don't think he'll show up, if others are here."

Halfway up the stairs, she paused, leaning on the railing. "Maybe Hayja can't control my mind. If he could, why wouldn't he simply make me dislike you?"

Daniel laughed. "He obviously can't. Now you're thinking rationally. He's manipulated you, making you believe that he could." He checked his watch. "Now hurry up. It's only eight p.m., but it's getting dark out there. I don't want you in the middle of a fight, so let's get going before he starts lurking around."

Mary nodded. "I'll be right down." She ran to her bedroom, grabbed jeans, tees, underwear and a nightgown, and shoved them into a backpack. In the bathroom, she added her hairbrush, toothbrush, powder, blusher and lip gloss, then headed down the stairs. "I'm ready," she said, clearing the last steps.

And saw Daniel, lying unconscious, face down on the rug.

Hayja stood over him, studying his fallen rival. Then he turned to her, a cruel smug smile on his lips. <You are a fool, Mary. Now your lover will suffer for it.>

"NO!" She rushed over to Daniel, pulling him onto his back, her hand on his chest. It rose against her palm, his heartbeat erratic. Red welts marked his neck and throat, and a swollen, purple bruise discolored his forehead on the right.

Hayja bent down to them. <Not yet dead. I want the pleasure of watching as he struggles in the throes of black water, of savoring his terror as my beloved sea floods his puny lungs. I want to see his hated body swell and bloat with death, a feast for sharks.>

"No, I won't let you! I know you're not what you claim to be now. But, Hayja, please don't harm him. If you've ever really loved me, please let him go. It's my fault that he got involved. He's not a part of whatever game you've played with me!"

<My affection for you has declined with your continual disobedience. Your lack of humility and your willful denial of my rights as husband have proven you unfit to be my mate. No woman ever refused me before, not once in six thousand years. Yet you, who refused the truth when I offered it to you, who instead worshipped your god of science and offered me its lies to explain my existence, you dared to disobey me and think yourself my equal. I play no game. I saw you, I wanted you, and I took you to mate. I spoke the truth to you at our first meeting, disguising myself but a little, knowing you needed that guise to satisfy your incessant questions. But nothing has satisfied you, neither the truth, nor the small lies I wove about it to soften it. Now I abandon both disguise and lies. You no longer deserve the kindness of deceit or the anesthesia of reason. Now know me as I truly am.>

Slowly his gills closed in on themselves and were replaced by smooth skin and muscles. His body transformed, growing taller, stronger, suddenly clothed in the mythic splendor she had painted him in.

<Yes, Mary. You called in your mind to Poseidon. He bade me, his third-born son, answer you in his stead. I found you fair and, with my fa-

ther's blessing, took you to wife, only to find you willful and rebellious and the wine of your love quickly souring. You betray me with this man, give him what I am refused, and now you plead for his life.> He glared at her so hatefully, she flinched. <But I will give you another choice if you are willing to bargain with me.>

She draped her arm protectively over Daniel. "Whatever you do, please don't hurt Daniel. Please!" Her arm shook, and she stared at it blankly, as if her brain, utterly exhausted, no longer controlled it. "Just don't hurt Daniel."

<Will you give your life for his? Both are equally worthless to me: an unfaithful, unrepentant mate, and an arrogant, mortal man.>

"If we're that worthless to you, then walk away from us. You've injured Daniel. You've had your satisfaction. Leave us in peace."

<I cannot do that, Mary. You have dishonored a god. Gods impose a harsh price upon those who have wronged them.>

"You never really told me that you were a god. You only asked if I would believe it. I thought you were teasing me. You never said anything more on it. Instead you lied to me, about yourself, about your people."

<I never lied to you, Mary. Do you recall your words to me that day? No? You said: *I don't believe in gods from the sea.* And I attempted to explain in a manner which you might comprehend. All that I told you was the truth. Humanity rejected the gods, ridiculed them, choosing more distant deities. They believed us worthless, dying or dead legends. And we did suffer, needing devotion to be whole. My people, the ancient ones, began to sicken. Many fell into a deathless sleep, unable to revive when humans abandoned them. The others who were spared this inertia discovered that they were sterile. The gods could no longer bear their own seed unless they lay with feckless humans. And then the children of these unions were mocked and reviled by humanity, and so we hid them from your kind, waiting until they replenished our numbers. One day they will restore our glory. Then we will confront errant humanity and demand its repentance.

<That day is approaching, Mary, and you might have helped its advent. You might have borne me a child, as my mother long ago bore me for my father. My other wives have, devoted and obedient to me, despite their children being taken at birth to be raised by other immortals, despite the fact that their own mortality would soon sever them from their children and from me. But if you will repent now and be a dutiful wife, I will destroy this man and forgive you your indiscretion.>

She smiled at him with a strange serenity, part faith, part sorrow, part madness. "I can't let you kill him and save myself. And I'm not a bed for your seed to grow in. Whatever you and your people may be, you are not my god, you are not my maker, and I will not bow to you."

Hayja scrutinized her pensively. <Then you choose to die. Come, Mary, I will hold you tightly as the sea takes your life. I will place your expired form in a wondrous cave in the farthest ocean depths, safe from scavenging predators, and dutifully entomb you in a sea cairn. You were once a good wife. I have not forgotten that.>

She knew her choice was final and stole one last glance at Daniel as salty tears began a silent and slow trek down her cheeks.

<Come. It is time.> Hayja extended his hand. She took it and stood up weakly, frightened, trying to muster her courage, knowing if she resisted, it would cost Daniel his life.

And her heart thought, not her mind, for she had filled it with a nebulous vacuum: *Good-bye, my Daniel. I love you.*

If Hayja heard its echo and timbre, he gave no sign of it.

* * * *

They walked to the edge of the star-lit shore, Hayja's hand still entwined in hers as if they were still lovers. He unclasped it and, in a fleet movement, swept her up into his arms, one arm around her back, the other under her legs, and carried her like a child, steadily into the sea. She wrapped her own arms around his neck, afraid but more afraid for Daniel, should she falter out of fear, and try to escape. If she did, Hayja would see to it that she died more horribly and would finish Daniel off as well. She had only Hayja's word, the word of a god who had forgotten that a human mother bore him, that he would spare Daniel, if she went quietly to her death instead. She had nothing else left and prayed that Hayja would honor his word.

Waves lapped frigidly at her back, hips and feet. Hayja's arms tightened, locking her against him, and she buried her head against his cheek and neck, her unchecked flow of tears bathing his skin. The ocean closed over her head and now his grip crushed her like steel. She held her breath instinctively, but there was no respite and her lungs and mind screamed in alarm and she strained against his arms frantically and uselessly. Her last thought rang out: *If you loved me, you would never have done this. Your heart has never known love, Hayja, for it has never sacrificed for it!*

Then only her desperate mindless inhaling for breath remained, the sea rushing in instead, her lungs and throat exploding, and her terror until black unconsciousness descended.

* * * *

Mary awoke, dazed, weak and confused, in darkness. Then, slowly, she became aware of the cool gritty dampness beneath her back, hips and legs, the hardness of the arm that cradled her head. Her eyes adjusted to the faint moonlight and she recognized the shadowed face of the man who knelt beside her on the damp sand.

Hayja.

Am I dead?, she thought.

<No.>

She struggled to speak, her throat raw and burning, and finally managed a rasping whisper. "You spared me."

<No.>

But I'm alive, her mind countered softly.

<Yes.> His head remained bowed, his figure silent as a statue, except for his chest. It rose and fell in staccato breaths as if agitated.

"D-Daniel…!" She cried out hoarsely.

<He lives.> A haggard strain permeated his telepathic voice. <My time is now short, and I must tell you that your challenge has been met. My father bids me tell you, but I need no prompting. You have won. Did you gamble on the pride of a god as you were dying, Mary, or the love of a god? Did my pride make you the victor, or my love?

<My heart had never known love, you said, for it had never *sacrificed* for it. Your challenge stung me, that all of the matings of my immortality, up to our own, were weak and selfish affections, less than human in the face of your own courage and sacrifice.

<And as your last breath flooded away and your mind and heart, too, began fading, your last emotion stabbed sharply into me: *you forgave me.* No words expressed it; you were beyond coherency. But its essence struck deeply, and I no longer wished you harmed. It shamed me and awoke within me a new judgment of you, that your willfulness and refusal to be subservient were a measure of your self-respect.

<No woman had ever been my equal, neither god nor mortal, until that moment. Suddenly you were beautiful and priceless in your strength that carried you past death. I had to accept your challenge, to love as selflessly as you have loved. Failing that, I would know throughout all eternity that you were not only my equal, but my better.

<It no longer mattered if you loved me. Your life, which I had taken, became more precious to me than my own and, without expectation or demand, I wished to make amends, to willingly answer your challenge, no matter how great the price.>

"But I'm not dead," she murmured.

<The gods have long decreed: if one life be restored, another must be lost.> He raised his head slightly so that she gazed directly up into his eyes. <I offered my own immortal life to Hades if he would restore yours. Hades heard my offer and accepted it greedily, foolishly believing my immortal life worth more than your precious and courageous mortal one. And my father and the gods heard Hades' acceptance and now they prepare to mourn

me. Sacrifice is acknowledged by the gods, and perhaps in that manner I will live on...>

"But you *are* alive. Perhaps Hades has spared you," she said, suddenly fearful for him, should he die and all he had learned die with him, and she would be guilty of having taught him how to sacrifice and of welcoming him into her heart and home before realizing her folly. And what must death be like for an immortal?

<I am no longer immortal,> he answered her thought, <but do not be burdened. I have gained a finer gift: I have loved unselfishly, loved another equally and greater than my isolated self.> He bent slightly, kissed her and lightly brushed her hair with his fingertips. As he released her, easing his arm from her gently, tears issued from his eyes, translucent and glistening in the moonlight, pattering softly down and moistening her upturned cheek.

<Good-bye, my only love.> He began to stand, one knee still bent on the sand, the other leg half-raised, foot pressing into the sand to hoist himself up. A look of surprise wrenched his face and he reached his hand outward towards her as if in supplication. Then his face and body stiffened as she reached out to grasp his extended hand.

It crumbled at her touch, no longer flesh, but sand. "Hayja!"

She stared in shock at the sand-sculptured man that had once been Hayja. Its unseeing eyes stared back at her, haunting her.

And then it collapsed, crashing in a shower of sand rebounded onto the damp and uncaring shore. A large wave rolled in, cascading against and past her, to wash over and reclaim its own, returned to the sea.

She stood up unsteadily, shivering in her wet clothing, and saw Daniel a few yards in front of her.

"I'm cold," she murmured, teeth chattering.

He walked over to her, put his arms around her. "I heard...it all. Saw it. There's nothing...no need to explain." They stared at the sea for a moment, a moment of silence, and then she leaned against him for support, as they walked slowly back to her house.

"He loved me," Mary whispered.

"Yes, he did," Daniel said. "Hayja...proved human after all."

"I died."

"No. You survived."

She slowed up and halted, and he waited. "We survived," she said, looking up at him, attempting a drained smile, then stared back out to sea, forever to be haunted by it.

"The gods will remember him," she murmured. "Take me home now, Daniel. I want to shower and to sleep, and I want you to stay with me."

He led her over the dunes and filled all of her requests.

She had no idea how long she'd been sitting there, reliving the past, when she heard Daniel's car pull up in the drive of their house in Carmel. The downstairs door opened and the voices of her husband, their ten-year-old daughter, Beth, and eight-year-old son, Tyler, drifted up to Mary's studio. She checked her watch: nearly five p.m. Time to start dinner.

As she rose from her chair, she glanced at the conch shell resting on top of the bookcase just below Hayja's portrait. She pressed her hand against it, as she had many times in the last twelve years. But it caused no tingle, no strange sensation. The magic that had powered it was gone.

SWING TIME

MAY 1939, FRANKFURT, GERMANY

The Swing Youth, dancing enthusiastically to the songs of Teddy Stauffer, Nat Gonella and Louis Armstrong, heard the music abruptly end. As the club door burst open, they bolted for the exits, but police swarmed into the rented dance hall, rounding them up.

Wilhelm shouted at one policeman yanking on his long brown hair and shoving him toward the trucks holding other kids inside. "Get your hands off me! Go kiss Goebbels's Nazi ass!" A second police officer, young but tall and muscular, helped the first, grabbing Wilhelm's other arm. They flung him into the truck.

The second officer growled back at Wilhelm: "You like to shake around like jungle monkeys? Break your stupid ears with that filthy music by American Negroes and Jews? You disgust me!"

Wilhelm stood up in the truck, whistling the melody to *Making Whoopee* snidely, his brown eyes defiant. He moved his body to the song and gave a rude imitation of the German salute, his fingers separating into Churchill's famous Victory sign. "Swing Heil!"

The incensed officer jumped into the truck bed, drawing his arm back and driving it forward rapidly. Wilhelm couldn't compensate fast enough to avoid the blow. The fist smashed into his mouth. It tore his lip and jarred his teeth. Momentarily stunned, he sank to his knees, the long key chain hanging from his hip clattering against the metal floor.

The policeman ripped Wilhelm's Harlem Club lapel pin from his zoot-suit and threw it back at him, jumping down to the street. He took a handkerchief the first officer offered him, wiping blood from his fingers while glaring back at Wilhelm. "Stinking *stenze!*"

Pretending to be too injured to rise, Wilhelm searched the truck bed for his lapel pin, found it, and clutched it tightly.

* * * *

As he pressed the ice pack against his swollen lip, Anna sat worriedly beside Wilhelm. His blonde-haired and blue-eyed Jewish girlfriend, they would never have met if her family had been orthodox, but her parents were assimilated with many Christian friends. Now the few friends remaining to the Saltzmans were helping them flee Germany. "Wilhelm, with my family leaving Frankfurt tomorrow, I must go home soon and pack tonight. We have our visas and we can't delay another day. Follow us, Wilhelm. Come to New York."

"You want me to run like a coward? Most of my friends, they don't like what the Nazis are doing to Jews, but we don't have to leave. You do. Your family is at risk, but I'm not." He stared at her, his mouth still swollen. "I'm glad you weren't there last night. God knows what would have happened to you. Yes. You and your family must get away quickly, Anna, even if it means losing you for a while. But I'm not in the same danger. What can they do? Send me to the Labor Front? Let me stay here and defy them. They've taken everything good in life and distorted it to their own lies. I want to find a way to resist them, to help us outlast them."

"They can send you to a camp. I've heard this."

"That's a risk I'll take. You go to America. I'll write to you. Try to eventually join you there."

She took the ice pack, drained the excess water, and recovered the cloth around it. "Here. Put this back on your lip. You'll also need to have that tooth filed down." She took his hand. "Do you really love me, Wilhelm?"

She asked it quietly.

He answered as quietly. "Yes, I think I do. I suppose we would have been better off never meeting."

"But we did meet. It happened. Tomorrow, if my family gets away without mishap, I'll worry about you for months to come. Promise me you won't fight the Nazis so visibly. You were lucky the police let you go. Stop making yourself a target. I need you to survive."

"Survive."

"Yes. This time will someday pass. If the future is kind, Germany will come to its senses, rid itself of Adolf Hitler. But the Nazis won't let you win while they're in power. Don't fight. Just survive." She pressed a sheet of paper into his hands. "This is my aunt's house in Hoboken, New Jersey. You'll always be able to find out where I am from her. I have your address here, but we don't know if my letters will reach you." She shook her head as if their troubled world could not be fathomed. "We have little time left. I keep thinking I'll never see you again."

He raised his hands, cupping her face. "No more swing." He kissed her in a lopsided, closed-mouth way. "I hate the world."

She kissed him back carefully, avoiding the cut on his lip. "But it will keep turning. There will be time enough for swing later."

"Promise?"

"I promise to hope for it."

He went to his dresser, picked up his lapel pin, and gave it to Anna.

"Then take this with you to America. The bastard ripped it off me tonight, but I found it. When I join you in America, we'll swing together again." He pulled her back onto his bed, caressing her.

NOVEMBER 1982

When Benjamin reached his twenty-first year on October 9, 1982, his mother, Sarah Ellman, and his grandmother, Anna Saltzman, presented him with a marvelous gift: a month's tour of Western Europe. Bubie Anna made one request of him. He was at City Hall in Frankfurt, Germany to fulfill it, the last stop on his itinerary.

He spoke German fluently and carefully explained his inquiry to the Records Clerk behind the desk, who now scanned records on strips of microfilm through her viewer. "So your grandmother, Anna Saltzman, was secreted out of Germany with her parents and sister in the spring of 1939, and she waited to hear from your grandfather who had stayed behind?" The comely girl, her dark brown hair pulled back neatly into a bun, looked up at him. "And she never heard from him?"

"Yes, that's right. She wants to know what happened to him. She's convinced Wilhelm Haupp would have contacted her if he could after the war."

"Well, I don't see his name listed here. Let me try the archives. They go back further." The girl searched through files in a nearby cabinet, pulled out new rolls of microfilm, and brought them to her desk. She threaded them into her viewer, her hand turning its wheel to read each document. After a few minutes, she paused. "Yes, here he is, Wilhelm Haupp. Oh!" She pursed her lips, reading the magnified data on the screen. "I'm sorry to tell you this, Benjamin, but your grandfather died in 1940."

"Was he sent to the war front?"

"No." She shook her head, regarding him somberly. "Wilhelm Haupp committed suicide on March 3, 1940. He threw himself off the Eiserner Steg—the Iron Bridge—and drowned in the Main. I'm so sorry to be the one giving you such bad news on your first trip to Germany. You probably expected to find him alive."

Benjamin stared down at the floor, then up at her. "Yes, and tell him about my mother, that Anna Saltzman had given birth to his daughter after arriving in New Jersey." He glanced at her. "Does it say where he jumped?"

She nodded. "In the middle of the bridge. Look. My shift ends in ten minutes. I feel so bad telling you this. If you don't have any other plans, would you like to go to dinner together? My name is Lotte."

Benjamin hesitated. "Actually I'd first like to go to this bridge, to where Wilhelm died, and say a prayer for him, if you don't mind. After that, dinner sounds great."

She nodded again. "I'll be happy to take you there, and to go to dinner,

Benjamin."

"Ben."

"Okay, Ben. Just let me put the microfilm away and close up my office. After we visit the bridge, I know a wonderful little café where they serve very good sausage, and other dishes, if you don't want traditional German fare. And the beer is always flowing." She cleaned up, turned off her equipment, then put on her coat and grabbed her purse. They headed out into the autumn evening.

* * * *

"The Eiserner Steg," Lotte said as they climbed up onto its span. "A pedestrian foot bridge, built in 1868." From what little Ben knew of bridge construction, it appeared to have a long travel deck, and two tall cantilevered arches rose up like towers a third of the way past either bank. Each arch dipped downward to meet gracefully in the bridge's center point. It was all gray metal with a handrail with a flowerlike circular design below its sleek horizontal handgrip. But tonight it represented the loss of the man Ben had hoped to meet. Tonight, he would pray for the lost soul of Wilhelm Haupp.

He was glad he wore his heirloom: the badge from the Harlem Club of Frankfurt Grandfather Wilhelm had belonged to, a rectangular white metal lapel pin rimmed in blue. Wilhelm had given it to Bubie Anna on the night they parted. A keepsake, he had told her, a promise to swing together again. But they never had. "I guess we'll walk to the midpoint. I don't suppose we know which side he flung himself from?"

Lotte shook her head as they continued along the bridge. "It didn't say which."

They reached what they hoped was the middle spot where Wilhelm had ended his life. Ben reached out to Lotte with his right hand. "Would you mind holding hands with me while I say my prayer?"

"Not at all." She grasped Ben's hand and they gazed out at the waters of the Main.

"Wilhelm Haupp, may your soul find rest knowing we wish you had a happier ending to your life." Ben raised his left hand, his fingers touching the white and blue lapel pin from the Harlem Club of Frankfurt. "You gave Anna Saltzman this pin in the hopes that you would swing together again when the war ended and the world regained its sanity. I would ask God, if it is in any way possible, to someday reunite you with Anna again. Until that time, I pray that your soul finds a way to be at peace, knowing you were loved. Amen."

"Amen," Lotte echoed. She drew her hand away from Ben's. "You weren't holding my hand very tightly, but it feels like it's tingling."

"Both of mine also have a numb tingle. In fact, it's spreading to my arms."

"Do you think the temperature has dropped suddenly, chilling us?"

"I don't know. It does feel colder. But now that I've said my prayer, I think we can have our dinner as planned. Let's get off this windy bridge and head for the café you told me of."

"All right." She led him over the Eiserner Steg to its northern bank. "I know a short cut." Lotte pointed down a long residential street, its houses crowded together. They continued walking. Daylight quickly faded and dusk descended on the neighborhood.

They turned one corner, then another. Finally, Lotte stopped, looking confused. "It should have been right around this block. Right here." She gestured at an old-fashioned florist shop, its lettering done in a fancy script. Lotte checked the street sign. "This is the right street. Funny, though, I don't recall this nearly medieval lettering."

"It's weird," Ben said, "and it's gotten dark so fast. The street lamps seem weaker, the few I'm seeing. Maybe we're on the wrong block." Ben gaped at a car moving slowly past them. "That's a vintage car. It's got to be at least forty or more years old. Either that or it's a reconstruction. Probably a reconstruction. Looks too new."

"Yes. It must be. Let's go another block. It should lead us back to the avenue."

It did, Ben noting other vintage autos driving past them. "Is Frankfurt hosting some kind of historic auto show?"

"Not to my knowledge. It is strange." She pulled her coat tighter around her blouse and skirt.

"There's a café on the next corner. Is that it?"

Lotte shook her head. "I know where I'm at, but nothing matches. I've never seen that restaurant before."

"Well, we're hungry, so we might as well try it." He offered her his arm, glad he was decently attired in a double-breasted suit. The place might have a dress code.

It was a charming little café, soft lights providing an intimate glow. They were seated at a center table for four. They looked over the menus and gave their orders to the waiter.

"Those were very strange prices," Lotte remarked. "Beyond inexpensive. I've never seen such low prices."

"Maybe part of some historical reconstruction event going on, and you've just been unaware of it. Got your nose stuck in that microfilm all day."

He grinned at her as three boys and one girl, perhaps 17 years of age or so, came boisterously in. All dressed smartly, the boys wore loose suits, baggier at the hips and tightened at the cuffs. The girl, her auburn hair sleek and long against her shoulders, her lips sporting a bright red lipstick, wore a knitted pullover, a skirt and heeled pumps under her unbuttoned coat. They swiped two extra chairs from a nearby table and grouped themselves around Ben and Lotte.

"So who's the new chick, Wilhelm?" the tallest youth asked.

"I'm sorry," Ben said carefully in German. "I believe that you're mistaking me for someone else."

The second youth, shorter and a bit pudgy, poked Ben's arm. "Come on, Old Hot Boy, what are you trying to pull with that fake American accent? I mean, Anna's gone. What's the problem? So you have a new girl." He turned to Lotte. "I'm Fats. Are you hot, Swing Doll?"

Lotte shook her head. "No, it's quite comfortable in here, right now."

The newcomers stared at her then laughed so raucously, Lotte blushed. The arrival of their meals saved her from further questioning. The third boy, who seemed the oldest, said, "Let Wilhelm and his new doll eat their supper. We'll see you at the dance. *Heil Hottler,* Wil. Watch out for the Hitlerjugend Patrols. They've been up and down the town like good little Hitler *schmucks.*"

"Oh, yes!" Fats laughed. "We appreciated Anna's teaching us that word. The Hitlerjugend are pricks!" The redhead gave him a disapproving glance, but he ignored her, taking money from his wallet. "Waiter! Their dinner is on me!" He handed the frowning waiter a few bills. "Tip included. What are friends for, Bill? See you later."

They started toward the door, but the redhead held back. "It's good, Wilhelm," she said to Ben. "It's good that you have a new girl. What's her name?"

"Lotte," Ben answered for her, looking at her nervously.

"Treat him kindly, Lotte. He lost someone he loved over a year ago. He almost went *meschugge*—that means 'crazy'. Can I tell her, Wilhelm?"

Ben said nothing, just shrugged and nodded.

The girl leaned on the table, toward Lotte, lowering her voice. "Anna Saltzman and her family left Frankfurt and went to America. They were Jews. They faked their identification papers and got false visas."

Ben looked up at her startled.

"Don't deny it. Wilhelm's letters to her were never answered, sent to her aunt's address in America. The aunt wrote back that Anna had died in an automobile accident when her parents, sister and she were driving from New York to the aunt's house in New Jersey. Wilhelm has been so depressed over this, I'm glad to see you here. Help him to get over Anna, to accept her loss."

Ben sat stiffly and silently as the girl gently squeezed his shoulder and smiled at Lotte. "See you at the dance, Lotte. I'm Gerdy, and those fellows are Roy, Fats and Teddy. Well, not actually, but those are their nicknames. Wilhelm is Bill."

She joined the others as they waved and left.

Ben and Lotte finished their dinners silently, drinking their beer uneasily.

Lotte leaned toward Ben. "They think that you're Wilhelm Haupp."

"Who's been handed an immense lie by someone. My grandmother and her family made it safely to Hoboken. And I think we have a much bigger problem."

"Yes."

Lotte beckoned to the waiter. "Do you have today's newspaper?" He brought it over to her. She and Ben stared at it, dumbfounded. Its logo had the same archaic lettering. Its date was March 3, 1940.

"My God!" Ben said.

Lotte shivered, her eyes huge with alarm. "Well, at least Fats generously paid for our meal. I doubt that our cash or credit cards would be recognized."

Ben, his alarm matching her own, whispered, "Wherever Wilhelm is, he's destined to kill himself tonight. Whatever brought us here, whoever's running this show, means us to stop him. We have to go back to that bridge and quickly!"

Lotte breathed in heavily and let it out. "Let's go to the restrooms first. I doubt the opportunity will come again." She frowned. "Just in case something out there scares us even more."

Ben nodded.

"And then out into the cold dark night to find your grandfather and try to prevent his death."

Ben got up slowly. "Okay. Meet you back here in a few minutes."

* * * *

The night grew colder. Both were glad for the warmth of their overcoats. They passed more than one house displaying the Nazi flag and photo of Hitler, making Benjamin wince with both horror and sorrow. Bubie Saltzman had lost family to the Nazi butchery. And tonight, unless they could prevent it, she would lose the man she called her first true love. Ben wondered, if he and Lotte did stop Wilhelm's suicide, would it make any difference? Would they even get back to their own time to find out? "Lotte, I'm really afraid."

Lotte fumbled for his hand and clasped it in her own. "Are you religious, Ben?"

The question threw him. "I never considered myself to be. I mean, I believe in God and some kind of destiny. But maybe—after tonight—it's not absolute, not unchangeable."

"I'm a devout Catholic. I believe everything in life is God's will. He knows everything, but doesn't tell us what role to play. We have to choose. Our free will guides us to make the right or wrong choices."

"And how does that relate to *this?*" He gestured sharply at a Nazi flag.

"And I'm asking myself why I'm taking this journey with you, Ben."

He suddenly stiffened. "Lotte! Down the next block! Look at those kids, their armbands!"

She looked. Heading their way were five youths, wearing brown shirts with a black scarf fastened around their necks with a ring, short black pants with white knee length stockings and brown shoes. On their left upper arm, an armband prominently displayed a black swastika against a light square.

Grimly and calmly, Lotte removed his vintage lapel pin. "I recognized this pin from Holocaust courses. It's the emblem of the Frankfurt Swing Jugend. They were almost as hated by the Nazis as the Jews. Those boys are Hitler Youth. I'll hide this pin in my purse, Ben. Let's walk quietly down this side street." She linked her arm through his. "It should lead us to the river Main, which should still have shops and promenades. Maybe we'll lose them."

They moved away from the five teenaged boys.

Lotte squeezed his hand to reassure him. "You don't look Jewish. People can't really tell." She chanced a glance back over her shoulder. "Oh, no! They're following us. Keep walking! We're just a couple, out for a stroll."

"Hey, you!" The five boys had sped up and the biggest one confronted them rudely. "Where are you two going? You don't look local. In fact, you look rather strange. Are you foreigners?"

Ben and Lotte turned slowly to face them. "I'm visiting Frankfurt with my friend Lotte here. We're going to stroll along the Main. If you don't mind, we'll continue on our way now."

A short pudgy boy snorted meanly. "Just visiting? Maybe he's a spy. Maybe he's a Jew! Let us see your papers! We don't believe you!"

"Please," Lotte murmured, "leave us be. We were not bothering you." She tugged on Ben's arm, looking at him. "Come on, Ben."

The tall bruiser deliberately pushed between them, separating them, and he and the four other boys surrounded Ben. They began to riffle through his overcoat and suit pockets and the tall one pulled out Ben's wallet, opening it up. "Let's see if you have something worthwhile in here."

Ben stood frozen. "Give me that back!" He reached out to take it back but the blond-haired boy held it away and three of the boys grabbed Ben, holding him immobile. Lotte's one hand covered her mouth in fear and her other hand reached out to the assailants. "Please, don't!"

"Shut up, fraulein!" The blond leader opened up Ben's wallet, pulling out his driver's license and a small stack of German and American currency. He stared at them in confusion. "What is this joke?! This license is American and dated 1979 and your money is also dated years from now. Are you a counterfeiter?"

The short boy peered at Ben's driver's license held out in the tall one's hand. "Look at his name. Benjamin Ellman. I think he's a Jew. Let's turn him in!"

The tall brute pulled out Ben's social security card. "He's a Jewish spy. This card's fake, too. Says he was born in 1961." He turned to Ben, appraising him. "Do you want to explain this, Jew boy?" he asked snidely.

Despite his fear, Ben felt anger rise in him, fury for these bastards and their contemporaries who would be responsible for the deaths of twelve million innocent people. If he was going down, he was going to tell them the truth. His voice stayed steady as he spoke. "You don't know who I am or what I am, but I'll tell you where I'm from! I'm a time traveler, from the future, from 1982! And I came to tell you that you're all losers! You and Hitler will lose the war and go down in history as the monsters you became!" He noticed the grip the three Hitler youth had on him loosened and one boy let go, walking away, saying: "He's crazy. If we bring him in, they'll think we're crazy for believing this idiot."

The blond boy eyed him warily. "What's an American from the future doing here now?"

"Ask God," Ben countered, shaking off the other two boys. "Lotte is also from the future. Lotte, give him some coins from your purse. Show them the dates!"

She fished out two and handed them to the leader of the youth. He studied them, frowning. "They're both crazy."

Lotte opened up her hand for the coins. "Let us alone and we won't tell anyone you saw us. If our superiors know we've been discovered, they'll want to eliminate you."

He dropped them into her palm as if they were burning. Then he took Ben's wallet, license, card and money and flung them down into the street. "You're both lunatics." But his voice shook. "Maybe they have ray guns."

Ben smiled. "We left those back in our time machine. Want to see them?" He wore a smirk.

The boy looked at him, perhaps afraid that Ben and Lotte were telling the truth or if not, that their madness was contagious. "You're a lunatic and a liar." He faced his friends. "Come on. I don't want the Hitler Jugend thinking we're crazy, too. Let's go. Maybe they'll drown in the Main."

He turned back to Ben, suddenly leveling a hard punch to his face, knocking him down. Another kicked Ben viciously as they all laughed raucously, insulting him, and turned to leave.

The small heavy boy turned back briefly, shouting, "Hitler will win. You go tell the future that, you lunatic!" The big blond boy grabbed him roughly and yanked him along, running away from Ben and Lotte.

Ben got up slowly, rubbing his leg which was sore but intact. He quickly retrieved his wallet and its contents and returned it to his coat pocket. His breath came heavily out, frosting the air. He touched his tender cheek and jaw, sure that a bruise would soon be blossoming there. "You were brilliant, telling them they might be eliminated! Straight out of a sci-fi film. Thank God they left!"

Lotte took a ragged breath. "Just following your surprising lead, Ben. Which apparently worked. But we intimidated and humiliated Hitler Youth. They might come back. Let's get to the bridge." They walked on quickly, shaken, and reached the Main. Other people meandered along its banks. They headed back to the Eiserner Steg. The bridge spanned from its northern to its southern banks, its architecture stately in the gloom.

They climbed up and headed to the middle of the bridge. In the distance, two other couples were exiting it on the farther side. Lotte turned, facing him. "Ben, why did Anna wait until now to find out what happened to Wilhelm?"

Ben sighed. "Because she married another man. She loved Wilhelm and wrote to him, hoping to reunite, but it was wartime in Germany. She never received a response, and six months later, her aunt's daughter, her cousin Sophie, introduced her to Morris Ellman, a good and decent man.

"Morrie fell in love with her, and even though she was nearly seven months pregnant, he wanted to protect her and give her coming baby a father and a name. Being an unmarried mother was considered shameful in those days. Still, Anna held off for another month or so, hoping she'd hear from Wilhelm. She was nearly nine months pregnant when she finally accepted Morrie's proposal. They were married in a small private ceremony in the Rabbi's chamber.

"When my mother Sarah was born, Morrie insisted on raising her as his own flesh and blood. My mother was only told the truth when she turned twenty-one years, and then she only told me two years ago, after Zayda Morrie died. He had a stroke. He was seventy-eight years old, eighteen years older than Bubie Anna. She's only sixty, still full of life."

Lotte nodded, "I understand now. She couldn't try to contact Wilhelm while Morris was still alive out of propriety and respect for him."

"Yes. That's exactly what she said."

"What will happen if we prevent Wilhelm's death?"

They leaned over the bridge railing. Ben shuddered as the weak night lamps shone on the cold waters of the Main. "I don't know. And how in the world will we get back to 1982?"

"We're in higher hands," Lotte murmured.

"Lotte, what's on the other side of the Main?"

"Taverns. Splendid apple wine." She smiled at him ruefully. "But our money's not good."

He pulled out his wallet, examined it. "Nope. All dated wrong."

She smirked unhappily. "We'll have a glass if we ever get back."

"So where is Wilhelm? Could that be him?"

He glanced back to where they'd entered the bridge.

A lone youth walked toward them. When he reached them, he and Ben gazed at each other with shocked expressions.

"Are you Wilhelm Haupp?" Ben asked softly. The nearly identical young man eyed him incredulously. Lotte grasped Ben's arm, shivering against him.

Wilhelm Haupp nodded, his expression sad and perturbed. "Who are you? How do you know my name?"

Ben swallowed, forced himself to breathe evenly. "I'm a relative of Anna Saltzman."

"Anna? She's dead."

"No, she's not dead, Wilhelm. She wrote to you, but you never wrote back."

"I never heard from her. No letters. Who *are* you? Why do we look so alike?"

Lotte took the lapel pin of the Harlem Club from her purse, handing it to Ben. He showed it palm-up to Wilhelm. "You gave the pin to Anna. She gave it to me. She sent me, umm, here to find you."

"Who *are* you?" Wilhelm asked again.

And Ben, still in shock, answered truthfully: "I'm your grandson, Benjamin Ellman."

Wilhelm shook his head, smirking. "How can you be my grandson? I'm only seventeen. You look like me, but what you say is impossible."

"Yes, sir, it is." Ben kept thinking: this is my *grandfather.* "But it's also true. Anna sent me to Frankfurt to find you after her husband, Morris Ellman, died...in 1980, two years ago. I met Lotte here in your city in 1982. It was 1982 just a few hours ago when Lotte and I somehow walked into Frankfurt in 1940."

Wilhelm stepped back. "You're crazy."

"We may sound like we are but we're not."

"Ben," Lotte said. "Show him your money!"

Ben nodded. "Yes! Yes, we can prove it. Look at our money, Wilhelm." Wilhelm kept backing up as Ben put the pin back into his trouser pocket and took his wallet out.

Lotte reached out to Wilhelm, her fingers spread in an imploring gesture. "Please! Let him show you."

Ben handed him his wallet. "Look at the money inside." Wilhelm pulled out the mark notes, some German and American coins, and a few American dollar bills Ben hadn't converted. "There are traveler's checks, but you wouldn't understand them."

Wilhelm moved into the scant light of the bridge lamp and peered closely at the dates on the bills and coins. He put them back into Ben's wallet. "They are all dated far in the future. If this is a prank, it's an elaborate one. So…assuming by some miracle this is true, then I never received Anna's letters and she never received mine, the few I sent, because her aunt deceived us and lied to me? That Anna didn't die in an automobile accident, that *that* was a lie? And that she married another man and took his name and gave it to her child? My child also if you really are my grandson. Was the child your father or your mother?"

"My mother. Sarah Ellman."

"And your grandmother is now Anna Ellman." He laughed as if conversing with a madman. "So why am I not an old man in 1982?"

Ben hesitated. "Her name is still Anna Saltzman. It's the one thing she asked of Morris Ellman: that he let her keep her maiden name legally. Socially, she let them call her Anna Ellman, but officially she stayed Anna Saltzman."

"Why? And again I ask: why could you not find me as an older man in Frankfurt in your future? Oh, I know. I *died*. Right?" His voice dripped with sarcasm. "I don't know who put you both up to this, but you shouldn't seriously expect me to believe it. It's extraordinarily cruel of you."

"Wilhelm Haupp, I'm sorry you would think that of me. I'm trying to explain despite these very frightening circumstances. My grandmother insisted on not changing her maiden name in case you someday tried to locate her. She hoped one day to learn that you survived the war and, even though she committed herself to Morris, she could privately tell you about your daughter, that one day you could meet her and her children. She also said you promised each other you'd survive 'to swing together' again." He was close enough to Wilhelm to see his pupils dilate, a gesture of surprise. "As far as why we couldn't find you in Frankfurt in 1982, when Lotte looked you up in the City Hall records…" He floundered.

Lotte put her hand on Ben's shoulder, then grimly faced Wilhelm. "Wilhelm Haupp, it is a mortal sin to commit suicide. God sent us back here for your sake as well as Anna's."

"What? What are you talking about?!"

Lotte frowned at him, her eyes hard. "How were you going to kill yourself tonight?"

Wilhelm wore so horrified an expression that Ben wondered if the modern records were wrong. "Lotte, maybe it was an error. Maybe Wilhelm died accidentally, and the authorities only thought it was suicide." He looked at his grandfather-to-be. "Maybe we can prevent whatever was going to happen, and you can go to America and find Anna." He paused, still studying Wilhelm's face. "You're crying."

Wilhelm shut his eyes, tears coursing down his cheeks. "I was going to drown myself tonight. Now I'm not. I'm going to go home, and I'm going to survive. But I will not contact Anna Saltzman for a very long time."

"Why?" Ben asked, confused.

"Because everything must be as it was, don't you see, with the exception of my not dying. You must come here in 1982 to find me. Otherwise you will not find me in 1940, and I will not survive tonight to hopefully live into your time." He smiled sadly. "If God has performed a miracle tonight to change my life, I must not upset God's plans. If Anna and I are to meet again, we'll let God arrange it." He glanced at Lotte, then Ben, and sighed heavily. "But if all of this is true, I hope someday to find out why Anna did not receive *my* letters, and why her aunt told me she had died, a terrible deceit."

"I don't know why her Aunt Magda lied to you. It may have been because Anna was Jewish, unwed and pregnant by a Catholic boy an ocean away in Germany. People can act cruelly to avoid social scandals and preserve a family's dignity. But Bubie Anna told me that she waited until the last possible moment, hoping you would find her, before she married Morrie."

Lotte turned to Wilhelm. "Are you going to be all right?"

Wilhelm regarded her solemnly. "Yes. I promise you both. Are you his girl?"

Lotte shook her head. "We only met this afternoon."

"Then you were meant to meet. I only wish that there was some way you could prove all of this, that I am not imagining it all and have gone *meschugge.*"

Ben regarded him sadly. "May I please have my wallet back?"

"Of course."

Wilhelm handed it over, and Ben began riffling through an inner compartment. "Ah, here it is." He brought out the two old photos, carefully protected in small plastic sleeves. "This is Anna's picture when she went through Customs, right after she arrived in New York, and here is another with my mother as a newborn in Anna's arms. That's Morris behind her. She asked me to show them to you, if I found you."

Wilhelm reluctantly gave him back the photos. "Benjamin, you and Lotte need to get back to your own time, and I must get back to my life.

Thank you both for saving it."

Ben put the photos away with shaky hands and slid the wallet back into his pocket. "Wilhelm, we don't know *how* to get back."

"What did you do before you crossed into 1940?"

Ben frowned. "We came to this bridge, to the spot where you jumped to your death. And I was wearing this pin you gave to Anna before she left."

He took the white metal rectangular pin with its blue trim from his pocket again. "The Swing Youth emblem. I touched it in remembrance and it made my hand tingle. Lotte was holding my other hand. I said a prayer to you and suddenly the tingle spread, and Lotte also felt it in her body. It was weird. We walked on, crossing the bridge to the northern bank and found ourselves in 1940. I have no other explanation."

"You walked here, guided by something greater than the laws of nature. Put the pin back on, hold hands, and walk back."

"Which way?"

Wilhelm considered. "I think you should continue across the bridge to the southern bank. Look, here are three two-mark coins. If you're still in my time, at least they will buy you each a glass of apple wine to calm your nerves. Just walk. I don't know how to guide you beyond that." His voice softened. "I hope to see you both in the future." He held out his hand, clasping Ben's and then Lotte's. "I go the other way. Goodbye and good luck… and thank you."

He slowly turned, heading to the northern bank, then stopped, looking back at them. "Tell Anna I loved her."

Ben nodded. "I will if we meet in the future. I hope you tell her yourself in person."

Wilhelm smiled and continued on.

* * * *

Ben put the Swing Jugend pin into his lapel and took Lotte's hand. "Do you want to say a prayer?"

She nodded. "Silently. Each of us." She shut her eyes and he shut his, praying for their safe return to 1982.

They left the bridge and walked quietly along toward a tavern. Lotte squeezed his hand. "If it doesn't work, at least we can get a glass of apple wine."

An almost imperceptible shimmer lightened the night sky. The Main, the Eiserner Steg, and the streets seemed suddenly brighter. A car came down the street. A modern car.

Lotte's tears finally came. "Oh, my God! We're back!" She wrapped her arms around Ben, burying her wet face against his chest as her body shook.

He clung to her tightly, just as weak and relieved. They held each other up, waiting until their shock and tremors passed, and unsteadily made their way to the nearest tavern. They seated themselves and ordered apple wine.

They sat for a while sipping the wine, letting it soothe them.

Ben had paid for their bottle with a traveler's check. He handed Lotte the three silver marks Wilhelm had given him in 1940. "We didn't dream it."

She smiled as she put them in her purse. "We must check the records tomorrow to see what happened to Wilhelm."

A portly older man approached their table. "Excuse me. Is your name Benjamin Ellman?"

"Yes, I'm Ben Ellman."

The gentleman's face sported some lines and a slightly-doubled chin, but he appeared to be in robust health. His eyes riveted Ben's. "And this is Lotte with you." He leaned in toward them and spoke in a near whisper: "I am not going to repeat this, because only we three know it's true. No one else will believe you both were somehow transported back to 1940 and saved my life on that bridge. But however you traveled in time, you have my deepest thanks for stopping my suicide. And I, as promised, made no attempt to contact Anna so as not to disrupt the timeline with your visit this year to Germany, which brought about our miracle. So we must pretend from this point on that we are meeting for the first time tonight in 1982."

He straightened up and spoke in a normal voice: "May I join you now?"

Ben nodded and Wilhelm pulled out an empty chair at their table, sitting down. "Today's events surprised me and told me everything had probably come around full circle, even before I took the chance that you both had returned safely and might be in this tavern near the bridge." He explained further. "I received a phone call earlier from your grandmother Anna. She said she'd had a chance meeting with one of my colleagues in America this week and discovered that I was very much alive and well. She said she had sent you to try to find me here in Frankfurt, Ben, and gave me the address of your hotel to contact you, but you were out when I called. When you do return to your hotel, you'll find a message from Anna telling you to stay put. She is already on a flight to Frankfurt for our reunion." He signaled the waiter and ordered another glass of apple wine for himself, then smiled at Ben. "Anna said I would be surprised at how much you resembled me at your age. Of course, I already discovered that in 1940. Anna also said you might be wearing the Swing Jugend lapel pin, the one I gave Anna over forty years ago, which she handed down to you, Ben, my long-lost grandson." The waiter brought his apple wine. Wilhelm lifted his glass in a toast. "To new beginnings." Ben and Lotte gazed quietly at him, and then lifted their own wine glasses, clinking them with Wilhelm's, echoing his toast in a chorus: "To new beginnings."

They all sipped their wine.

Wilhelm reached over and touched the Swing Jugend pin on Ben's lapel, examining it. "You know, Ben, your Harlem Club pin is in excellent shape. You must wear it tomorrow as well. When Anna arrives, she insists that we all go dancing."

TINY DOLL-FACE

The house loomed before her, cold and sepulchral. "So I'm finally, formally, invited to visit with your mother. Remarkable, the power of a small gemstone." She waved her ring finger in the sunlight; the diamond's facets flashed.

"She's still not happy about it, Doll-Face."

Sarah ignored his favorite sexist endearment. "It's high time you stopped letting your mother run your life," she said as he led her to the parlor.

The gaunt woman in the wingback chair surveyed her with an uncertain but dignified scrutiny. Her hair, dyed black, was pulled back into a twist, her face thin, but her eyes dark and sharp. Sarah smiled at her, determined to be pleasant. "Hello, Gertrude. How are you?"

"Not well, but managing. Wally knows my back can be sore. Just sitting for more than half an hour is a challenge."

More likely stiff, *that back of hers,* Sarah thought, *from that rigid attitude.* She stared around the room, noticing all of the dolls. "What a stunning collection."

"Some of them are quite rare," Gertrude informed her. "Take that small Egyptian doll. A grave doll, done in the image of a servant who would serve the deceased in the afterlife. And the tiny crude figure beside it is a voodoo doll, made in the likeness of a victim, whom the magician wishes to control or kill."

Sarah swallowed and sat closer to Wallace on the sofa. "I prefer the modern dolls."

"No doubt you played with those fashion floozy dolls as a child."

"Uh, no. I never owned one of those. I liked paper dolls." She changed the subject. "Wallace has told you we've set the date."

Gertrude nodded, as an older man came in, wheeling a tea trolley. "We'll have tea now. Alexander, please pour. This is Wally's Uncle Alexander. He lives here as well."

Alexander bent over the trolley and fixed them each a brimming cup. It was fragrant and warm, and Sarah sipped it, taking the edge off the chill in the room.

"Yes," Gertrude said, "Wally has told me of your wedding plans. I personally can't imagine his moving from home and hearth, but he seems bent on having you, and I know of only one way to please his desire. More tea?"

Sarah held her cup out. "Then you'll give your blessing to the marriage."

"Sarah," Wallace cut in. "That is my place to ask."

"Then you ask," she returned, quickening anger making her stomach queasy.

"Mother, will you accept Sarah into the household?"

"Yes, dear. But, of course, there's no need for you to leave home to do so."

"Wait," Sarah piped, surprised and disgruntled that the word had come out in a tinny squeak. "We're not living here. He's a grown man. We need a place of our own, Gertrude."

Gertrude shook her head, a crafty smile playing on her lips. "But he belongs here. And done our way, my dear, not even death will part you from him." And then she mumbled, a string of guttural sounds, nonsense words.

"You're impossible," Sarah said. "Wallace, let's leave. I've sorry, but my patience is exhausted." She started to rise. She heard Wallace reciting his own hodge-podge of gibberish, as a dizzy spell hit her. She sank back into the chair, seeming to fall into it.

She had no memory of blacking out, but when she awoke, her limbs felt stiff and she was laying naked on a bed, in a darkened room. Wallace was beside her, fondling her. His hands seemed much larger than usual, and she wondered if she was sick with fever, imagining it.

He reached over her and turned on the bedside light. Sarah gazed up at him in horror. He had doubled in height and the shock caused a scream to rise in her throat. But her mouth would not open, even when her line of vision took in the shelf of dolls. Each had its own name plaque: Ruth, Karen, and Beth. The empty space read *Sarah*.

"Mother knows best, tiny doll-face," he cooed at her and kissed her lips, forever frozen in a fetching pout.

TRICK OR TREAT WITH JESUS

Sister Miriam hated autumn. She knew the good Lord saw fit to color the trees in a blaze of red, yellow and orange, but so did He color the flames of Hell. It was appropriate, a warning to all good Christians. Halloween was coming, and she hated Halloween, the Devil's own holiday, and nothing holy about it.

Miriam trudged over to the bus stop, lugging her "Repent, Sinners, or Suffer Everlasting Torment" sandwich board. She had added biblical verses to the backside board, exhorting the lost souls to accept Jesus as their savior. When she got on the bus, dropped token and forty cents into the box, and was handed her transfer, she blessed the driver. This one didn't say thank you. He would roast, oh, sweet Jesus, he would roast. She could tell which ones would fail on Judgment Day.

The bus took her, as always, to the elevated train, the transfer bought her passage, and she rode above ground until the train descended into the tunnel beneath Center City Philadelphia and brought her to 15th Street. Her major audience awaited her there, those sinful commuters, leaving their jobs, going home for the day, thinking of mortal concerns and pleasures and nothing more. Well, when she finished with them, they might open up the bible instead of turning on the TV.

She got off the train and positioned the sandwich board around her body as people pushed by her, boarding the train. Miriam was feeling particularly fine about her calling. That morning, as she read her own bible, opening it randomly to see God's special message for her, the passage had blared: "Make a joyful noise unto the Lord."

Miriam needed no microphone or bullhorn. The noise she was capable of making was well-known in Center City. And they couldn't stop her. She was in the Lord's service.

She took a deep, lung-stretching breath, and her voice covered the enclosed station like a net seeking fish.

"YOU'RE ALL GOING TO HELL!"

* * * *

When the fish—or commuters—dwindled to a trickle, Miriam crossed the overpass to the other side of the tracks. The train pulled in, half-empty at 7:00 p.m. Miriam stepped in, took off her sandwich board, and sat down.

At 2nd Street, a young white man came on board and leaned near the door, ignoring the available seats. He spoke out in a moderate, calm voice. "Excuse me, people. What would you say if I told you I've brought a bomb on this train, right here in my knapsack?"

Miriam checked him out: olive green pants, white short-sleeved shirt, clean brown loafers. He carried a leather jacket in his hand. The knapsack, same color as the pants, rested on his back. He had short blond hair, neatly combed, a thin face and skinny body. He wore silver-framed glasses. He didn't look like a terrorist.

The other people on the train ignored him, but Miriam caught a few worried looks among their faces.

"If you were going to die," the boy said, "right now, would you be ready to face God? Have you lived a life in the service of your Maker if a bomb went off on this train? Could you face Jesus and be welcomed by Him into Heaven?"

A woman two seats down turned to a girl next to her and said, loud enough for others to hear: "Just what we need after a hard day's work. Someone trying to push their religion on us with scare tactics."

The boy took this as a call to arms—rightly, Miriam thought, although she hoped he was joshing about a bomb. Never could tell with folks today.

The boy looked at his challenger. "The Lord says I am the light and the way. Follow me or burn in the fires of the Beast." The woman stared back at him, defying him and denying him, another sinner, as sure as Jesus died for our sins. Miriam watched her pull a book out of her tote bag and open it to some page tagged by a bookmarker. It sure as hell wasn't the Good Book. Then the woman spoke, louder than before, but she wasn't shouting. An actress's voice, that's what she had, and it carried: "We are *all* God's children. The only sin here is the sin of pride, pretending you know which of those children God loves." Then she went back to reading her book.

It was more than Miriam could bear. She rose up, dragging her sandwich board over to the woman. "The Good Book tells us which ones Jesus loves," she bellowed. "Good deeds will avail you nothing. Good intentions will fling you into the pit. Only accepting Jesus Christ as your savior will bring you to the promised land." The woman cast her eyes at her, one brow arcing, then continued to read. Miriam felt a shaking rage build in her heart. She wanted to smite this unbeliever, but she knew the law. She could only wish she'd see this woman writhe in Lucifer's lava pits, boil in the volcano that awaited her.

Miriam walked over to the young man. "Jesus will reward you for speaking the truth." She lowered her voice now, speaking only to him. "Let the Devil take them if they won't believe."

The youth smiled at her. "God will reward me indeed very shortly." He looked at his watch and spoke softly now. "It's due to go off in about seven minutes."

Miriam stared into those cool grey eyes. "You don't have to play around with me, son. I'm a believer." The kid just stared back at her, calm and certain of grace. Miriam repeated, "I'm a believer. But it's up to God to punish the sinners, boy, not us."

The young man slowly shook his head. "It's war. The only way to teach those who defy Jesus." He turned slightly away from her, his face determined.

Miriam stared at his knapsack. "You gotta teach them the right way. Like every Halloween, those kids come, and I give out Chick pamphlets, to get them on a path to Jesus."

The youth checked his watch again. "Five minutes."

Five minutes. It would take her at least eight to her stop. "I hope you're not crazy, boy."

He turned back to her. "Aren't you ready to meet Jesus?" His tone taunted her. She stared at him and dragged her board over to a seat and sat down.

Three more stops to go. She glanced at the kid, but he was staring out the window, his back with the bulky knapsack turned to her. There was maybe two minutes left if he was serious. Not enough to make it home. What was in his sack? Did he really have a bomb?

The train pulled into Allegheny station, slowing down. Miriam picked up her sandwich board and got off the train.

The woman who had sassed her, the girl beside her, and the kid with the knapsack all looked at her on the platform as the train doors shut and it pulled away.

Miriam watched it disappear down the track and stood there waiting, waiting for the explosion, but none came. She cursed the grey-eyed kid then, a tool of the Devil, trying to tempt her through mortal fear. What good was she to Jesus dead? The dead can't preach to the sinners.

* * * *

The little pamphlets were stacked on a card table, set up near the front door. They told the story of Jesus, and the stories of those who had rejected the Lord and the punishment they suffered for their willful ignorance. They told how to get salvation, and how not to fall into the clutches of the false religions.

The doorbell rang, and Miriam answered it.

A boy dressed as a Ninja and a girl done up as a flapper from the Roaring Twenties greeted her. "Trick or Treat!"

Miriam took two pamphlets from the table. "Ain't no devil to do tricks here, and the only treat is saving your soul for Jesus." She dropped one pamphlet each into their bags. "God curses Halloween. You kids go home and find Jesus."

The children stared at her, then down at the pamphlets in their bags. They turned, disappointed, and left her house. Going to some other house, looking for devil's food to rot their teeth and souls.

She dropped more pamphlets into more outstretched Halloween bags, exhorting the children to abandon the witches' sabbath and seek the Lord. A few kids bad-mouthed her, but she stood there like a rock, unmoved, unwavering. One little girl insisted that Jesus already loved the little children. Miriam told her sternly, "Not when they kiss Lucifer's backside on Halloween. He's looking to snare you, girl, to take you to Hell and away from Jesus!" The child started crying, and Miriam thought perhaps the girl saw the error of her ways, but her friends drew her close and whispered to her, and the girl spat "You're crazy!" at her. Another lost one.

Around 10:00 p.m., the doorbell stopped ringing. Miriam began to put the rest of the pamphlets away. She locked her door and sat down in her easy chair, lifting the bible off the end table beside it. She opened it randomly to the 24th Psalm. "To you I lift up my soul, Oh, Lord, Oh, God. In you I trust; let me not be put to shame, let not my enemies exult over me. No one who waits for you shall be put to shame; those shall be put to shame who heedlessly break faith." She stopped reading it aloud; the last line was troubling. The doorbell rang.

She put the bible down, grabbed another Chick pamphlet and unlocked the door to stare at the man outside.

He was dressed in a creamy white robe belted with a rope; his brown hair and beard cascaded down upon it. His brown eyes stared sadly into her own. He held an opened green knapsack in his hands, which he thrust forward at her. "Trick or treat."

"Trick," Miriam muttered. "You're a trick. Be gone from me, Lucifer."

The man didn't leave. "David also wrote: 'The sins of my youth and my frailties remember not, in your kindness remember me, because of your goodness, O Lord,' and 'For your name's sake, Lord, you will pardon my guilt, great as it is.' How could the Lord be as unmerciful as you paint him, Miriam?"

"You...you're the Lord? Did I die? Did I stay on that train and get blown up?"

"You got off the train, Miriam. You had to wait for another one to complete your journey. Nothing exploded."

"You're not real. You're the Devil tricking me." She tried to close the door in his face, but he held out his hand. He didn't touch the door, but it moved back, out of her hand, opening fully up.

She peered at him, and that's when she saw the others, the creatures behind him. One looked like a human bat, another, a green ghoul; another was a shapeless mass with three eyes midway, watching her mournfully.

"You're the Devil!"

He reached out to the three-eyed thing and gently stroked its quivering flesh. "Do you think I or my father would turn away from those who seek us from a different pathway than your own? Or hate them because they do not bow before us?" He moved into her living room with the monsters, pushing her backwards as he moved forward. And from behind them, children in Halloween costumes entered, crowding the small room, holding out their bags to her. Their eyes cut into her soul, demanding, angry.

Miriam backed against the wall. "Lord, save me!"

"I cannot save you, Miriam. Save yourself. Empty your heart of pride and prejudice and arrogance toward the children of the Creator. You are not their judge."

One by one, the children began emptying their bags. Candy bars, boxes of candy, lollipops, gum in balls, sticks and chicklets, jawbreakers, popcorn balls, apples, candy corns, marshmallow pumpkins, gummies shaped like worms and other wriggly things both sweet and sour, pretzels, potato chips and pennies began to pile up around Miriam.

Jesus spoke again as the wall of Halloween treats rose around her. "Even in the depths of Hell, where souls have lost their way, does the true Creator of all life reside and send spiritual succor to its inhabitants, so they might follow a thin thread of hope. How can a father abandon children, no matter how errant? How can a father deny creations who seek a different mode of praising him from other creations who have decided what that mode shall be? And who are you to decide another creation's path to his, her or its creator?"

The Halloween treats pillared up around her eyes. The children floated to the top, building her a prison of sugar and starch. And now they drew Chick pamphlets from their bags, raining them down on Miriam. The small space between her, the wall and the mounds of treats began filling up with the booklets. "Please, dear Lord! Forgive me, forgive me, forgive me!!!"

Silence. The cheap paper tracts stopped fluttering down on her. "Jesus? Jesus? You still there?"

No answer.

Miriam pushed at the mountain of goodies surrounding her. She tried to climb up it, but the treats she stepped into avalanched, tumbling down into the cushion of Chick pamphlets, knee deep around her. A second attempt buried her to her waist.

"Jesus! Jesus? God! Is anybody there?!"

She gave in to a couple of good crying jags over the next hour. Her body ached with weariness from standing up, stuck waist deep in the Halloween treats, but she feared sleep, feared falling into them, being suffocated.

She finally reached out and picked up a chocolate bar, slowly unwrapping it. She ate it slowly, then carefully lifted an apple from her Halloween prison cell.

Eventually she fell asleep, wondering if asphyxiation by treats would be painfully slow or painlessly fast.

Outside of Miriam's world, the trick-or-treaters were now asleep, some with the lingering taste of sweets on their breath. Their parents had checked their booty and put the good stuff away to be doled out over a reasonable period of time, saving their children from extra cavities and extra pounds. And inevitably, those parents snitched a candy or two, knowing their kids wouldn't mind, would let them taste a treat of Halloween and so remember their own pleasure in this night when they were young. On this night when the gates between the dimensions are opened and all manner of spirits can visit our world as if they'd never left it.

THE WAY TO A MAN'S HEART

Lorelei Tuscarelli wearily climbed the staircase leading to the Department of Arcane Literature at Miskatonic University. She had spent a good hour shopping that morning, trawling through the quaint shops of downtown Arkham, specifically for a woman's most significant bit of apparel: lingerie. The Massachusetts winter had subsided sufficiently to let her abandon her flannel nightgown; warm as toast though it was, it couldn't entice her husband to provide any extra human warmth in their king-sized bed. Professor Anthony Tuscarelli preferred to curl up with a compelling book, fiction or non-fiction, rather than his wife.

Hence, Lorelei decided that, with the onset of spring, it fell upon her to spice up their love life. She found the perfect strapless boudoir gown, black lace across the padded brassiere that would lift and shape her bosom and below it, sheer black silk flowed to her ankles. To further stock her sexual arsenal, she also purchased perfume advertised to drive a man wild with desire, and a bottle of scented lubricant. These she tugged in designer shopping bags as she reached the landing and trooped down the hall to her husband's office. Students passed her coming and going. Some of the young men gave her raven hair, blue eyes and perky smile appreciative glances. Not to mention her shapely legs. Lorelei still possessed a short but comely figure and pretty face for a woman of thirty-five.

She knocked twice on the brown wooden door with its frosted glass and turned the knob and entered. "Tony, darling. I thought I'd stop by and see if you're free for lunch. Hope you don't mind."

Professor Tuscarelli slowly raised his eyes from the term papers he'd been reading and marking. He stared at her fish-eyed, unblinking, then lowered his gaze to his students' papers again. "Lorelei, you can see I'm busy."

"You're always busy, here and at home. Has it occurred to you I might want a bit of attention as well?"

Tony Tuscarelli slapped his marking pen down on his desk almost truculently, pushed back his chair and stood up. "Lorelei, we're heading toward the end of this year's school term, which is always a hectic time for both teachers and students. My own forté involves imparting the mysteries of unique literature rarely seen outside of Arkham and seeing that my students understand all the religious, sociological and exotic components and references."

Lorelei studied him and wondered, not for the first time, how such an attractive man (with such rich brown hair, hazel eyes and noble patrician good looks) cared so little for the pleasures of his trim body and spent most of his waking hours only engaging his sizeable brain. In the four years since he and Lorelei tied the proverbial knot and moved to Arkham to accept the university's professorial position, she was lucky to lure him into the proverbial sack once a month. Didn't anyone tell him that it was legal to do more than snuggle the rest of the month? "Honey, I'm sure your students think you're the most diligent teacher in the world. But I think state law allows for lunch and break times, and what better way to spend that time than with me, your lonely honey wife." She sat on the edge of his desk as she described herself, leaning provocatively over so that the cleavage of her breasts peaked out from her low-cut blouse. She also mentally changed her self-description from "honey wife" to "horny wife" and hoped Tony was just a tad telepathic. Maybe all those strange books he read and taught about would help him read her mind. He obviously was bad at reading her lips, no matter how many nightly verbal hints she sent his way.

Neither mind-reading nor lip-reading worked this afternoon. He came around the desk and put his arm firmly around her. "I had a snack mid-morning and won't want lunch for at least another hour. Plus I'm bogged down with work. I've always said you need to find ways to engage your mind more during the day." He waved at the bags she had dropped on the office floor. "Shopping certainly isn't food for thought, Lorelei. If you're not going to seek a job yourself, you should read more. Why don't you stop by the library here at Miskatonic and find some books to intrigue you and keep you occupied until I get home this evening? They have a wonderful selection on a wide variety of subjects. I'm sure you'll find something to suit your fancy, dear." His arm had started to warm her and she'd thought of leaning in for a kiss, but he led her to her shopping bags, picked them up, handed them to her, and opened the door, ushering her out the threshold. "I'll see you tonight."

She placed her free hand against the door before he could close it behind her. "You'll be home on time?"

"I'll call you if I'm delayed. Now go to the library. Your library card is one of the perks of being my wife!"

She nodded absently as he did shut the door, his tolerant smile receding behind it.

Lorelei clenched her fists, trooped down the hall and down the stairs. *What the hell*, she thought as she headed toward the library. *Maybe they'll have something racy. Sheesh! What's the use of being married if you have to get your thrills from a book?!*

* * * *

The Miskatonic University Library, an early 19th century monstrosity, boasted a main floor, two upper floors, a basement, and a sub-basement reportedly filled with more books, countless periodicals and dated ephemera carefully stored to keep them from disintegrating. She walked crisply around the first floor, perusing the fiction section. While there were modern novels by 21st century writers cloistered around older volumes from the 20th and previous centuries, the only romances were literary. Not one sported a steamy cover with scantily clad men and women. Not that Lorelei was uneducated. She had read fiction literature during her college days and managed passable grades in English, but her BA in Business Administration and subsequent employment as a manager in a real estate firm in Boston hadn't quite prepared her for life in Arkham with Tony. They met when she was twenty-eight and Tony was thirty and teaching at U. Mass, Lowell. A three year courtship cumulated in his proposal of marriage and his landing the new job at Miskatonic at the same time. They weren't exactly prudish before marriage; Tony was more than sexually adequate, but both his new job and the atmosphere in Arkham seemed to create a creeping reticence in him when it came to the marriage bed.

She sat down at one of the tables dejectedly, glancing at a librarian seated at the information center, a woman not much older than she was, if appearances were any indication of age. The librarian apparently noticed her as well, turning a quizzical face to Lorelei, getting up from behind her desk and walking toward her. The woman's apparel smacked of dowdy collegiate style, long brown skirt and saffron blouse with white lace around her collar. Her light brown hair was pulled back in a low ponytail that hung to the middle of her back.

The woman paused beside her. "Pardon me, but you looked a bit lost perusing the shelves. I'm Mrs. Perkins, the reference librarian. Is there a specific book you were searching for?"

Lorelei warmed to her friendliness. "Not really. My husband works here and was too busy to have lunch with me. He suggested I take out something to read and go home."

"Who is your husband, if you don't mind my asking?"

"Anthony Tuscarelli. He teaches arcane literature."

"Ah, Professor Tuscarelli," she said with a knowing smile. "I know most of the professors. He has a reputation for being a bit of a workaholic."

Lorelei leaned on the table, lowering her voice. "Do you have a minute to talk, woman to woman?"

Mrs. Perkins sat down in the chair next to hers. "Of course, dear. How can I help?"

Lorelei took a deep breath and let it out. "Well, Tony hasn't, shall we say, been paying proper attention to me for the longest time. So I thought I might get him to notice me tonight using this." She opened one of the shopping bags and drew out the sheer black nightgown. "And other things." She drew out the perfume and lifted its cap, allowing Mrs. Perkins a sniff.

The librarian's smile became softer and sympathetic. "Well, you may turn his head with such things, but I've always subscribed to the theory that the best way to a man's heart is through his stomach. Have you considered greeting him one night with a romantic but gastronomically delightful dinner?"

Lorelei's face clearly reflected her doubt. "I'm not much of a cook. We buy a lot of prepackaged and frozen meals." She frowned. "Especially lately, he's been working till all hours and coming home long after I've eaten my own dinner. He just pops something in the microwave for himself on those nights."

"You poor dear, you look positively miserable. Why don't I show you our culinary section? It has some wonderful cookbooks and many are exotic enough to turn the head of a man in love with arcane knowledge back to his wife."

Lorelei shrugged. "I guess it's worth a try." She got up.

Mrs. Perkins also rose. "Wonderful! Follow me." And led her past the shelves marked Literature, Biographies, and Creative Arts, to a section marked Culinary and Homemaking Crafts. She raised her right hand and her fingers trailed across the spines of the books, resting on one and pulling it from the shelf. "Now you don't want just any ordinary recipes to achieve your goal. I'd say the professor would prefer a meal of mystery. This book might just provide the perfect menu." She handed it to Lorelei. The title read: *The Gastronomicon: Recipes to Enchant and Enlighten Discerning Palates.*

Lorelei scanned the Table of Contents, full of unusual names, reading one aloud. "Byakee Steak with Sautéed Mushrooms. Umm, he's not too big on beef. Prefers chicken and fish or seafood."

Mrs. Perkins peered at the contents over her shoulder. "Well then, how about Shoggoth Soufflé. It can be made as a main course or as a dessert. And if he likes seafood, try Deep Ones Delight."

Lorelei turned to the page for Shoggoth Soufflé, a lightly baked dish made fluffy by beating egg whites into white sauce along with fish, cheese, egg yolks and other stranger ingredients. It didn't look difficult to make but she had no idea what Shoggoth powder was or where to find it. "What is Shoggoth powder?"

Mrs. Perkins sighed. "There might be some ingredients in the cookbook that require a visit to The Arkham General Store downtown. They specialize in those unique additives."

"Is it safe?"

"Oh, yes, my dear. It thickens the soufflé…or the soup. I noticed there is a recipe for Shoggoth Soup as well in there. I'm sure Professor Tuscarelli will find either dish fulfilling."

"All right, I'll take out this book and try these recipes. I can stop by the Arkham General Store on my way home." She grinned. "I remember passing it when I went to the Enticing Undies store. Thanks for helping me, Mrs. Perkins."

"You're welcome, dear." She whispered, "Between us girls, perhaps you can wear that nightgown after dinner to see if it brings out the beast in him."

Lorelei giggled. "If it does, I'll come back to thank you again."

She waved goodbye, checked out the cookbook and went to the store for the shoggoth powder. Its box had the curious description "guaranteed to expand any dish exponentially to the 3rd degree." She furrowed her brows and decided against asking the clerk to explain that, murmuring: "Hope that doesn't have anything to do with the oven temperature!"

* * * *

At their quaint cottage along the Miskatonic River, she opened the kitchen windows to let in the breeze and sat at the table, perusing the book further. It certainly had some strange recipes, including one called A Sense of the Past with "Essential Saltes," and a back section filled with Middle Eastern recipes with "Abdul Alhazred's Favorites." She decided to leave those alone and simply cook the Shoggoth Soufflé, using salmon as its base, since Tony enjoyed that fish.

She preheated her oven to 375 degrees Fahrenheit and got to work. She made the white sauce and let it cool. Separating the yolks and whites of four eggs, she added the yolks one at a time to the white sauce with seasonings and then the salmon. She beat and whipped the egg whites with her mixer until they stood in peaks. Now it was time to add the shoggoth powder, the special ingredient. She opened the small package and peered inside. It was a fine white powder with little specks of green and pink mixed in that almost resembled little eyes. The recipe called for three tablespoons sprinkled liberally over the beaten egg whites. The powder looked festive on the whites, which she then folded into the sauce with her rubber spatula. Lorelei poured the completed mixture into her soufflé dish and placed it in her preheated oven to bake for the allotted thirty to forty minutes.

She was rather glad that she had stocked the kitchen with cooking dishes and utensils when they first moved to Arkham, having made some home-cooked meals in the early days of their marriage before his work pushed their relationship to the side lines. But she was equally glad that she had also picked up some broccoli and a cherry pie today at the general store for veggies and dessert. Just getting the soufflé cooked properly took all of her late afternoon energy. It was done and apparently successfully by 5:30 p.m.

She picked up the kitchen phone and dialed Tony's office to let him know she had prepared a special dinner for them. To her surprise, he was pleased and said he would be home in twenty minutes. Lorelei set the table, steamed the broccoli and put a chilled bottle of rosé wine on the table. She had been saving the wine for a special occasion and this seemed an apt time.

As Tony came in the door, she was placing the broccoli, rolls and butter, and the soufflé on the table. "Well, this certainly looks scrumptious. What caused you to cook us a feast for a change?"

"I visited the library as you suggested and found a unique cookbook, honey. I hope you like the meal. I made a salmon soufflé."

* * * *

They sat back, sated by her cooking and pleasantly buzzed from the wine. Tony belched. "My word. That soufflé was rather filling. And had a strange but satisfying taste I can't quite place."

Lorelei smiled. "That was probably the shoggoth powder, Tony. The dish is called Shoggoth Soufflé and uses three tablespoons of the powder blended into the egg whites."

"Shoggoth? Come now, that's a reference to a literary creature created by a famous local author. It's described as a shape-shifting, gelatinous, giant amoeba with eyes, mouths and pseudopodia. I doubt that shoggoths are actually involved in this recipe or in that powder."

"It's a white powder with green and pink specks in it. They do look a little like tiny eyes." She giggled, the wine making her light-headed. "They actually sell the powder at the Arkham General Store, along with ordinary veggies and fruits and baked items."

"And no doubt the container shows a monster on it, a tourist-trap item for fans of horror literature. Well, no matter. I hope you're going to continue cooking as delightfully as you've done today, dear."

"How delighted *are* you, Tony?" She had risen and was clearing the table.

He glanced up at her as she began soaking the dishes, glasses and cutlery.

"I can clean up later. I have another surprise for you, honey, but I have to put it on in the bedroom. Are you game?"

He stood up and walked over to her, putting his arms gently around her waist, nuzzling her neck. "I have to admit I'm curious. Shall we repair to the bedroom? I'm feeling expansive this evening."

Lorelei met his lips happily and wondered if that shoggoth powder was magical.

* * * *

Professor Anthony Tuscarelli did *not* have his mind on books, arcane, modern or anything in between. That much Lorelei was certain of, the moment she appeared in the doorway of their bathroom wearing the black lace and silk nightgown, the perfume and carrying the scented lubricant. His behavior afterwards brought back happy memories of their honeymoon in the Caribbean Islands.

At one point as she was sighing and moaning from his hands and lips and other body parts, the lovely nightgown crumbled on the floor as she and Tony wrestled on the bed, she noticed a strange slithering sensation on her now naked body. It was far too long and thick to be his "little dancing man," her pet name for his manhood, but it played up and down her inner thighs, bringing her to an ecstatic peak as it changed direction and she cried out with surprised pleasure.

Later, as she rained kisses on Tony's body, she noticed the tiny eyes around his stomach as they watched her appreciatively, and saw the small tentacles caress her tenderly before contracting back into Tony's flesh to shrink within it, hidden from view. Tony groaned and reached out his hand to caress her face and neck. "Shoggoths," he murmured. "It seems they're real. I feel so strange, but they don't hurt, and I seem to be able to control them."

"Are you angry with me? The librarian said the powder was safe. Do you need medical attention?"

He hesitated. "I believe I could get used to them. Do they frighten you?"

"Frighten me? It's like you've grown built-in sex toys, honey. Mmn!" She bent down and her teeth nipped at his chest. The tiny green and pink eyes winked at her.

"Then I think we'll keep this development to ourselves. People for decades have said Arkham has some mystical qualities and the Miskatonic Library, some unique volumes that might not always be considered fiction. Up until tonight, I discounted such rumors. But starting tonight, we have to explore the possibility that fact may indeed be stranger than fiction here. I'll have to start perusing some of the library's ancient treasures more thoroughly. It will no doubt change my curriculum."

Lorelei nibbled at her lower lip. "Tony? I ate the Shoggoth Soufflé, too. How come I'm not sprouting eyes and tentacles?"

He laughed softly but with a maniacal edge. "Do you want to?"

"Not really. They wouldn't complement any bikini I wore!"

"Perhaps only the human male is affected. We'll have to explore the other recipes in this *Gastronomicon*. Perhaps there are antidotes to these side effects."

"Then you want to be cured?"

He reached out and turned off the bedroom lamp, pulling her close to him. She felt his hands, lips and other pleasant appendages begin to caress her body. "The night is young," he said. "Let's sleep on it, and see what dreams might come."

WHAT A WONDERFUL WORLD

It started with the comic book.

My husband Dean is the editor of a fantasy magazine and we attend science fiction, fantasy and horror conventions. Dean is dear to me, always will be, but he's convinced, as are so many others, that these stories are, well, *just fantasy.* But after that day in the dealer's room, I'm not quite sure we'll ever be able to live with such a sane outlook again.

At one table, they were asking donations for the Comic Book Legal Defense Fund. Of course, Dean donated and bought one of those underground comics that do their best to outrage narrow-minded people promoting censorship.

I love comics and was riffling through the pile, but they weren't quite to my taste, which runs to Conan, Amethyst, Super Heroes and anything that deals with the Devil or other mythopoeic figures. The one Dean bought had, as part of its cover story, a cute little female dog with a bright red ribbon around her neck, who could do a great impersonation of Mary Sunshine, and an ornery bear with tics on his ass. I admit that I have a prudish streak that makes me dislike satirical sex and violence, but we bought it to support the Comic Book Legal Defense Fund.

The next day I read the comic and found out the cheerful dog irritated the bear into violently *buggering* her (one could almost hear the song, "What a Wonderful World," from *Goodbye, Vietnam* being sung in the background) and then the poor dog came to worse and gross luck. I couldn't help it. I stood on my soap box and complained loudly about the comic.

"Well," Dean said, "bears do get ticks, lice and fleas, and dogs with positive attitudes trying to get them to look on the bright side of things are generally going to get crucified. In comic books and in real life."

"But why do they have to write and draw such things?"

"It's satire, Terry," he patiently pointed out.

"It's disgusting," I insisted. "The world is rotten enough. *Gulliver's Travels,* now *that's* satire. They're pushing the envelope with *this!"*

"Exactly the sort of thing they want to push it with. No one's forcing anyone to buy it. It's a matter of choice."

I wrinkled my nose in disgust, knowing Dean was right but still upset. "Well, please don't leave it out. I do have some normal friends and relatives who visit. Put it in your office under one of your magazine piles."

"All right, but we don't have to answer to your friends and relatives."

"Dean, I'm sorry, but I do. I may understand creatively, but it's so un-spiritual."

"You know, one of your favorite authors is a big supporter of the Comic Book Legal Defense Fund. We need to champion our right to creatively express putrilage and other blood-soaked horrors. Controversial subjects which artists and writers cross the border into often suffer censure."

"I know that. But why can't writing and art be spiritually uplifting and inoffensive?"

Dean raised an eyebrow. "Your gentle and cheerful manner may gain you an honest following of friends, and I do love you dearly for your kindness and concern, but please don't write fantasy if you want such a perfect world."

He sighed and removed the offending comic book from my delicate presence.

Dean thought I had an overly sensitive personality. He never believed that stories and art could be manipulated to create much more than words and images on paper. Up until then, I had hidden what my imagination was capable of from Dean.

But that comic still had me so upset when he left for work, that when he came home from his editorial office late that night, nearly midnight, he found a large brown bear asleep on our living room rug. As it shifted in its sleep, he also noticed the knotted blanket tied around its waist, crotch and butt and the bottles of Rid Shampoo and the plastic bucket sitting on the coffee table.

I heard him creeping up the stairs, no doubt hoping the bear stayed asleep and calculating what furniture we could move to hold our bedroom door closed while we dialed 911. But then that cute little dog, also from the comic, complete with its red ribbon, left our bedroom, trotted halfway down the stairs and smiled at Dean.

And she talked: "Hello! You must be Dean. Everything's all right. No need to panic. My name's Fluffy. Terry's been waiting for you. She misses you so. You don't know how lucky you are to have a wonderful wife like her! Why, look what she did for Bruno over there," (she wagged her paw towards the bear) "and for me." She turned and wagged her ass at him. She was wearing a hand towel converted into a diaper.

Dean managed a hoarse whisper. "Where is my wife?"

"Why, upstairs. Come on, Bruno won't hurt you. He's so relieved that the lice and tics are gone. Terry smoked out the ticks and then used that nice shampoo to get rid of his lice. Then she smeared a cooling anesthetic on his rump, and the poor bear felt so much better, he apologized to me at once for buggering me and fell promptly into the first peaceful sleep he's had in a long time."

"And she fixed you?" was all he managed to say.

"Of course. A douche and some rectal cream, which she happened to have on hand. An organized woman is worth her weight in gold."

I sucked in my breath and appeared, coming downstairs in my nightgown. "Uh, Dean, I know what you must be thinking."

He shook his head. "No, you don't. I don't even know what I'm thinking, except do we know a good psychiatrist, who's also cheap?"

I attempted to explain. "This is all because of that comic and you telling me that in the real world, bears and other wild animals suffer like that. And I kept thinking that I wanted to heal the poor bear. And, um, then suddenly here he was. And the dog, too, because I was also feeling so sorry for her. I told the bear, as soon as he's better, he has to go, but do you think we could keep Fluffy? The cats like her, and she's such a *sweet* little dog."

Dean shook his head again. "Terry…none of this is happening. We're in the grip of a dual hallucination."

"No, honey, we are in the midst of one of my created realities." She sighed. "It's happened before but I hid my talent, um, from you. The plight of these two comic characters made me lose my control. I wanted to cure their injuries and their dispute. So they popped into my reality, and since you walked in on it before I was done, you can see them now, too."

The bear snuffled awake and, avoiding putting pressure on his rear, sat up in a leaning posture. "Sorry for the inconvenience, old man," he said. "Your wife really has shown me the error of my ways. She suggests that I groom myself twice daily to avoid such indiscretions and enlist the aid of other bears to remove pests from my person."

"Uh, yeah." Dean turned to me. "Either this is the wackiest dream I have ever had, or you have a talent that we will have to keep well under wraps. I mean, what's next, Terry? Dinosaurs? Or don't you have any sympathy for them, extinction and all?"

"I wish you hadn't said that, Dean." I sucked in my breath again, nearly faint with fear as the small dinosaur with its wicked sickle claw appeared behind him, making a chittering sound.

Dean froze. "Which dinosaur?!"

"Velociraptor. Don't move!"

"I hope you've conjured him with a full stomach, including dessert!"

I prayed to whatever gods might hear me—could this creature I materialized actually harm us?

"Terry, dear, why don't you instruct the nice dinosaur on how to *behave?* Can you conjure it away?"

I gulped. "I…I don't know how to send them away. They usually fade on their own."

"Now would be a good time to try!"

I shut my eyes, concentrating, and opened them. "No good."

At which point Bruno the bear lumbered onto all fours then stood up menacingly and let out an ear-shattering *roar*. Dean ran like hell into the dining room and jumped on the table, looking back as the velociraptor, all four feet of him, took a flying leap at Bruno.

The velociraptor's sickle claw, aimed at the bear's stomach, sank into the voluminous blanket wrapped around his midsection, catching in the thick wool. The raptor lost its balance, crashing down on the coffee table, sending the bucket flying and crushing the bottles of Rid beneath its feathery but scaly hide. Bruno crashed on top of it, his bulk pinning the raptor beneath him. Bruno stretched his jaw wide and sank his sharp teeth into the dinosaur's neck, shaking his massive head until its neck broke. Their combined weight took its toll on the coffee table. The wood splintered and cracked down the middle.

Bruno slid off of the dead velociraptor, his barrel chest heaving. "Good thing I was here," he said.

"Uh, yeah," Dean agreed, climbing down from the dining room table. He looked at me. "Don't think of *anything!*"

"I won't!" I squeaked.

"Unless it's very small and utterly harmless," he added.

We all stared at the dead velociraptor. It began to fade before our eyes. The table straightened out, became whole again.

Dean's look questioned me as I came down the stairs to the living room.

"I didn't want it," I whispered. "I wished it away."

"Wish it *all* away," he said gruffly. "It would have been nice to show a *dead* velociraptor to the Academy of Natural Sciences, though."

"It wouldn't have lasted that long." I gazed at Bruno and Fluffy, still very evidently in existence. "Are you ready to go now?" I asked the bear. "Are you healed up?"

The bear stared back at me and then did the best imitation of bowing that a bear could. "I am fine, and I thank you, my lady."

I nodded and glanced at Fluffy, still sitting uncertainly on the stairs, who admitted in a sing-song voice: "I should have had more courage. I should have bit the nasty thing's leg."

"Everything happened too fast," I soothed her. "Do you want to go back to the, um, comic realm now? Nothing bad will happen to you. Bruno says he'll watch over you."

"I thought you wanted me to stay here. You said the cats like me."

I sighed and glanced at Dean. "You're not real." My voice held a trace of apology and regret.

"Only in your mind," Fluffy whispered, "because you cared so much."

"Maybe someone will read that comic," Dean cut in, "and do something to help wildlife. Horror has a purpose and so does satire. Terry, I won't pretend to understand what just happened, but aside from thanking Bruno for, uh, saving our butts," (the bear grinned and nodded back at him) "can you send him and Fluffy back to the printed page now?"

I nodded slowly. "I wish you both a happier comic life."

"Wait!" Fluffy climbed down the stairs to me, jumping up in a begging position. I picked her up and cradled her, accepting a sloppy lick on my cheek, then put her back down.

The dog trotted over to the bear as I closed my eyes. "Goodbye."

I heard Bruno and Fluffy simultaneously echoed their farewells as I opened my eyes and watched them fade from the room. The blanket, the Rid bottles and the bucket sat pristinely, unused, on the coffee table.

Dean covered the distance between us, put his arms very firmly around me and kissed me. He still shook a bit. "For sanity's sake, please curb that imagination of yours!"

"I'll try."

"Don't try," he insisted. "Do."

Things have been saner since that night. He did come home once to find a dark-haired warrior in a leather loincloth regaling me with stories of his exploits. Dean actually enjoyed that evening, once he realized that my mind had edited out any desire for me in the legendary character. He joined in our conversation, somewhat tensely informing the barbarian that evil gods and monsters really don't exist. The warrior nodded and answered valiantly, "Of course not. Not when I have my courage and the sharp bronze bite of my sword! I've killed them all!"

I don't think Dean will let me read his slush pile.

ABOUT THE AUTHOR

Her parents named her Marilyn Carol Brahen. But in 1969, a new friend mistook her first name so many times for "Madeline," he decided to call her "Mady," which she liked. Over the years, other friends spelled it six different ways. She eventually chose "Mattie" as her official nickname, and when she began publishing, her byline became Marilyn "Mattie" Brahen, keeping a promise to her father to use both her given and nickname in print.

Mattie loved literature since childhood and discovered the books by her favorite author, Ray Bradbury, at the Bushrod Public Library when she was thirteen, about the age she began writing her own stories and poems. But becoming a published writer was a challenging road and she earned her share of rejection slips. Discouraged, she wrote to Ray care of his publisher on September 23, 1986, wondering if she should give up writing and asking his advice. Ray wrote back to her on September 29th. He told her to keep writing for, after all, she did love writing so that is what she must do! He sent her Dorothea Brande's book, *Becoming a Writer*, inscribed to her with the words "Good Luck! Keep Going!" And told her he expected a progress report from her sent to him each Christmas and a copy of her first published book. In 1993, she met Ray in person at Forry Ackerman's convention in Crystal City, Virginia and got a hug of further encouragement, and in 1994, her first published story, "The Gift," appeared in *Marion Zimmer Bradley's Fantasy Magazine*. She and Ray continued their mostly Christmas correspondence for twenty years. She loved him as her literary "Papa" and on an envelope with his reply, he drew an arrow to the stamp of Edgar Allen Poe with the words: "My Papa."

Mattie also sings and plays guitar, performing both her own and others' songs, and is an artist as well. She also loves gardening and reading. She lives with her husband, author Darrell Schweitzer and their two current cats, Tolkien and Lilly, in Philadelphia, PA.

www.ingramcontent.com/pod-product-compliance
Lightning Source LLC
Chambersburg PA
CBHW020651180626
46816CB00003B/1223